MY PERFECT FAMILY

Khadijah VanBrakle

HOLIDAY HOUSE · NEW YORK

Family shouldn't have a rigid definition.

You'll know it when you feel it.

Copyright © 2025 by Lee VanBrakle
All rights reserved. No part of this book may be reproduced, transmitted, or stored in an information retrieval system in any form or by any means, graphic, electronic, or mechanical, including photocopying, taping, and recording, without prior written permission from the publisher. Additionally, no part of this book may be used or reproduced in any manner for the purpose of training artificial intelligence technologies or systems, nor for text and data mining. HOLIDAY HOUSE is registered in the U.S. Patent and Trademark Office. Printed and bound in May 2025 at Sheridan, Chelsea, MI, USA.
www.holidayhouse.com
First Edition
1 3 5 7 9 10 8 6 4 2

Library of Congress Cataloging-in-Publication Data is available.

ISBN: 978-0-8234-5486-0 (hardcover)

EU Authorized Representative: HackettFlynn Ltd,
36 Cloch Choirneal, Balrothery, Co. Dublin, K32 C942, Ireland.
EU@walkerpublishinggroup.com

CHAPTER
ONE

November

With my last class over until after Thanksgiving break, it should be a happy moment.

Instead, it sucks.

Because I already know what the holiday will look like: eating boxed mac and cheese with some dry precooked turkey breast, just me and Mom. It's our tradition, but it isn't very festive. Definitely not the same as a house full of loud, caring family. But I don't have one of those.

I'm sitting at the city bus stop. Even with my coat buttoned up to my neck, I'm shivering. After tucking both legs under me, my gloved hands pull a paperback out of my backpack. A fantasy novel, of course. My shoulders relax as I sink into its world.

"Damn, Leena. Do you ever stop reading?"

A sigh passes my lips.

I meet the gaze of Ray—the only boy in my Honors English class, and a major pain in my butt. "Raymond, move along. Don't you have some elementary school kids to bully?"

He sneers down at me. "Ha, ha."

Two Ford Fiestas—decorated with red, white, and blue streamers, filled with seniors—race out of the parking lot and down Candelaria Road.

"Why are you always alone? You're too cute for the 'Lonely Leena' nickname I have for you." He takes a step into my personal space. "We should get together during the break."

This dude has a serious listening problem. Every single time he asks, the answer is always the same. I glare. "I'm good."

The self-important smirk hasn't moved from his face. "Once you're seen with me, your social life will be on fire." He's wearing a pristine hoodie with matching joggers. My white cable-knit sweater is from my favorite thrift store. I'd pay the last two hundred dollars in my bank account to smear dirt on him.

I shift to the edge of the bus stop bench.

Before he can say anything else, a shiny gray Prius pulls up. The passenger-side window slides down, and the driver yells, "Ray, you had all semester to flirt. Let's go."

But he doesn't move. "You on Snap?"

He must be kidding. My mom tells me I shouldn't be afraid to talk to guys at school, but they *annoy* me. As I shield my eyes from the sun, this one gets my best angry stare. "*Goodbye*, Raymond."

"Your loss." Ray turns to his friend. "She's more into her book than me anyway, Mo."

The driver winks at me. "She has good taste."

Who's that?

Curly black hair. A cute smile. A handsome face. Whoever he is, I don't know him—him, I would've remembered.

Mo meets my gaze. "It's kinda cold. Do you need a ride?"

Great! Now my throat's as dry as the annual New Mexico drought. Maybe it would be okay. Maybe I should. I could talk to this one—not Ray.

Just then, a beat-up Honda I recognize pulls up. "Let's go, my girlie!"

I wave at Mo, then say, "Thanks for the offer."

The Honda's passenger-side door creaks as I yank it open. "Why are you here? I thought your French class wasn't over until three p.m."

My best friend, Deidre, cracks her gum. "We played corny games and sang 'Frère Jacques.' I knew every single line; thank you, Duolingo. After forty minutes, we were dismissed. Good thing, since your mom called me and asked me to pick you up."

I shove my worn paperback back in my bag. "Who's the problem child this time?" My mom wouldn't have wanted me back so quickly unless one of her daycare kids needed extra eyes.

DeeDee grins. "A colicky newborn won't stop crying."

"Ugh, got it. Let's stop at Satellite Coffee on the way."

I used to pray for siblings, but DeeDee might as well be my sister because she's at our house more than her own.

Other than my mom, she's the only family I've ever known. She lives with her grandmother, who spends more money at one of the local casinos than at the grocery store.

Meanwhile, my mom has never met a child she didn't try to feed.

Twenty minutes later, we pull into my driveway. The green-and-yellow ASIYAH'S ANGELS DAYCARE sign greets us from above the front door. My BFF follows me in, and we're hit with the scent of baby powder mixed with Goldfish crackers.

"Ma, we're home!" My half shout goes unanswered as I set down the drink carrier. Toys are littered around the open-concept living room. Without being asked, Dee shoves pieces of a block mountain into one of the plastic bins along the wall. She's a better daycare employee than me. "Show-off."

I drop my stuff on the couch and join in the cleaning effort, removing dried baby food from the high chair closest to the kitchen.

"Hi, girls. Did you have a good day?" My mom wanders out of her bedroom, dressed in her daily uniform—a pair of faded jeans and a lemon-colored polo shirt with "Asiyah's Angels" embroidered over her heart. "The babies are all down for naps."

I hand her a large latte, the edges of my mouth turning down. "Miss Connor is still the best teacher ever."

"For me? Thanks, Lee Lee—you spoil me so much, daughter. Why the sad face?"

"It sucks I won't have Miss C in the spring. She's moving out of the state."

"I totally agree. Any teacher who allows quiet reading time—for anything except hate speech and porn—is one of the good ones." She focuses on my best friend. "Deidre, did you have anything for breakfast this morning?"

The cleaning stops. DeeDee stares at me for help, her eyes widening.

Not missing a beat, my mom points to the fridge. "Right after the mess in front of you is taken care of, get yourself something to eat."

The loud wail of a newborn pulls my mom away, and then it's just the two of us again.

Before my best friend can say anything, I thrust my palm towards her. "Shhh. Don't even complain. She asks every time you're here. Just chew a piece of gum in the morning so you can tell her you had a snack."

DeeDee puts away the last block while glaring at me. "Not your best advice—aren't you the gifted one? You know I'd never dare lie to your mother."

"Don't start with the labels. English is my only AP class."

She walks past me, and yanks open the refrigerator door. "Anyway, anyway. What do you want to do tonight?"

5

I park myself at the kitchen table and grab my herbal tea from the drink carrier. "We could check what's playing at the dollar theater, then sneak in some Raisinets and Red Vines."

DeeDee sets down a bowl of chunky salsa and a family-sized bag of tortilla chips, plopping into the chair next to me. The strong scent of jalapeños and garlic attacks my nose. "If you include some Junior Mints, I'm in." A candy addiction is something we both share. She takes a long swig of her iced coffee.

As I sip my drink, my mind wanders back to the cute guy in the Prius. "Hey, you ever heard of someone with the nickname Mo?"

"I don't think so. Why?" Her crunching hasn't stopped, but I've had a ton of practice understanding her when she's eating. "Wait, was it a guy? Where'd you meet him? I'm listening—spill it!"

I snatch a chip out of her hand and chew on it for a few seconds of peace. "I didn't meet anyone, so there's nothing to tell. Raymond has a friend he called 'Mo' and I was curious about it."

"What are you curious about?" My mom approaches the table with a burp cloth still draped over her shoulder.

"Nothing."

DeeDee grins. "Your daughter asked me about a *boy*."

My best friend gets my best side-eye. "Ma, ignore her. Mo is just a friend of a classmate." Good thing I didn't use the word *cute* to describe him, or we'd be having a different conversation.

My mom doesn't have a single introverted cell in her body. I got all of hers.

My mother smiles at me. "Nothing wrong with curiosity. Sounds like the young man's name might be Muhammad."

I want to ask her how she knows that, but I don't.

"Is that all you're eating, Deidre?"

DeeDee runs her finger along the insides of the bowl and scoops the last of the salsa into her mouth. "I ate half the bag. Is there anything else you need me to do?"

Before she can take the question back, my mom spits out a lengthy list of chores for both of us. We spend the rest of the afternoon sanitizing every surface in our small two-bedroom house. Ugh. At least all the daycare kids are gone by the time we're sprawled out on the couch.

This will be my life over break.

DeeDee taps me on the shoulder. "Hey, Leena, I gotta make a quick appearance at home. My grandmother texted. She wants to lecture me about something before her Friday night trip to the Sandia casino. I'll be back by seven. Be ready, or else the candy is on you!"

I laugh in her face. "Do you expect me to pay for the movie too?"

DeeDee winks. "Which one of us has to pay for her own car repairs, insurance, and gas? Once we graduate from

Chavez and have our apartment, you'll see how hard it is." She rises. "Miss Asiyah, I'm done with everything you asked me to do."

"Thank you, Deidre," my mom says. "Have a ton of fun tonight and tomorrow. On Sunday, I need you both to help me deep-clean the carpet and set up things for the rest of the week. Together, we can keep Asiyah's Angels' five-star rating."

Then it's just me and my mom.

"Here." She pushes two twenties into my hand.

I raise my eyebrows. "What's this for?"

My mom tucks her wallet back in her purse, then drapes it over her shoulder. "For you and Deidre tonight. Maybe splurge and get drinks and food at the theater instead of smuggling in candy from Walgreens." She grabs her drugstore sunglasses off the coffee table. "I'm off to Costco for snacks, juice boxes, and disinfectant wipes. Enjoy yourself. Maybe smile at a cute boy or two."

Warmth flushes across my face.

"Ma, don't spend too much. You have a bulk-buying problem. We don't need two hundred Capri-Suns." Meeting her grin, I remind her, "Nothing good happens when a girl smiles at guys my age."

She taps my forehead with her index finger. "Don't go and get their name tattooed on your ass, but a friendly *hello* never hurts."

The second after the front door shuts, I rush to my room.

Since next Thursday is Thanksgiving, but the daycare is open until Wednesday, fun is limited to the next thirty-six hours. Afterwards, my time will be spent soothing crying babies, corralling six-year-olds at snack time, and distracting preschoolers so they don't redecorate our walls with crayons.

There's only one bright side. Deidre will be right here with me.

She turned seventeen this past January and is Asiyah's Angels' only official employee. DeeDee is great with kids. She takes way better care of them than I can. People who judge her for being older than other sophomores never got to know how great she is. It's not her fault her grandmother stuck her in an online middle school for two years and never cared if she passed any of the classes.

I grab a quick shower and change into my favorite CAN'T YOU SEE I'M READING hoodie and my go-to pair of faded jeans. I'm pulling my shoulder-blade-length hair into a ponytail as a new notification goes off on my phone.

Girl, I'll be there in less than an hour. Be ready.

After I send DeeDee a thumbs-up emoji, the front door slams.

"Leena, are you here? *Leena!*"

The clock on my Galaxy phone tells me my mom's only been gone for forty-five minutes. Not long enough for her usual Costco run. I step out into the hallway outside my room, and she stops right before barreling into me.

"Ma, what's up?" Her eyes are red and puffy.

Her shaky hands wrap around mine. "We need to get to the hospital—give me ten minutes to change." She's jumpy. Her gaze sweeps the house, but never meets mine.

"Did someone we know get into an accident?"

But my mom is already behind her closed bedroom door.

I have no clue what the hell is going on.

CHAPTER

TWO

November

I pace around the living room, picking up stray pieces of lint while I wait. After grabbing a mini water bottle off the counter, my mom joins me.

"Ready, Leena?" She's wearing a knee-length denim dress, and her dark auburn hair is slicked back into a tight bun.

Dazed, I follow her out the door and into the ten-year-old Subaru parked in our driveway. My heart's thumping in my chest. I click the seat belt around me and sneak a glance at my mom.

She still won't meet my eyes.

"I got a phone call from Samira, my father's sister. He had a heart attack and was rushed to Presbyterian in Rio Rancho."

Blinking back confusion, I stare at the woman who gave birth to me.

WHO?

She's checking all her blind spots, even glancing up at the rearview mirror—except she never looks at me. We back out of the driveway and speed down Comanche Road. I hear only a dull ringing in my ears.

"*W-why?*" Numbness spreads across my body but I get one word out.

We merge onto I-25 before my mom answers me.

"I don't understand your question, Leena." Her fingers have the steering wheel in a vise grip.

My forehead throbs. A developing migraine. I push past the pain.

"I have a grandfather and great-aunt? In this town? That I've *never met*? You told me—you said my dad died when you were pregnant with me. Was that a lie?" Anger shakes my hands. "You told me you didn't have family. You came up with our motto *No secrets, no lies*, but you've been keeping this from me?"

We pass each mile marker in total silence.

It isn't until we merge onto the Paseo exit that she answers.

"I'm...I'm sorry. My childhood wasn't a happy one. I ran away from home at sixteen. It's been more than a decade since we've seen each other."

Water clouds my vision. All I can hear is the rush of cars racing by us in the left lane.

"*WHY?* Why did you keep them a secret?" Nothing she says will make a difference, but I'm owed an explanation. "Whatever happened, I still had a right to know. How did your aunt find you?"

Mom's voice is stiff. "Samira saw one of my daycare flyers at the food co-op in Nob Hill. They don't really live in town,

Leena. They live in Santa Fe. To be honest, I never thought I'd ever see them again."

We make a quick right into the hospital parking lot, and she pulls into the first empty space.

"Leena, you're right, okay. I should've told you a long time ago. But right now, we need to get inside. My father is very, very ill."

My childhood dream of a big family fades like the setting sun. I had one, but I didn't know about it, and now it's losing a piece.

"Your dad passed away a few months before you were born. That is the truth. I decided to bring you up alone. Now...can we postpone the verbal flogging for later?"

With my stomach churning, and my heart bruised, I follow my mom through the emergency room doors. The strong smell of cleaner wrinkles my nose. I plop down into the closest chair and stare at a silver gum wrapper on the floor. She leaves the registration window and takes the chair to my right.

Silence is the only thing we share.

All the times I asked her about our family, she lied in my face. Just because I stopped bringing it up doesn't mean it isn't important to me.

"As-salaamu alaykum, Asiyah. Thank you for getting here so fast." A tall woman, wearing a loose black dress that hits her ankles, hair covered with a white scarf, stops right in front of us. A Louis Vuitton tote rests on her shoulder.

"Wa alaykum as salaam, Samira. How's my dad?"

My mouth drops open. I'm not sure what they said, but my mom's frown lines distort her pretty brown skin. The bright everyday gleam is gone from her eyes.

How come I didn't know my mom speaks another *language?*

The lady's blank expression stays in place. "Alhamdulillah, he's stable now. They only allow one person to be with him while he's in the ER. You should go in."

"I will." My mom finally makes eye contact with me. "Leena, this is your great-aunt, Samira. I'll be back." She squeezes my hand, then leaves.

That's it? That's the only introduction I get?

I always dreamed of meeting long-lost relatives...but now that it's happening, it's weird.

"Hello, Leena. I know this must be strange for you. You're already a teenager and we've never met. How old are you?" Samira's tone is brusque.

"Hello, ma'am. I'm sixteen and a sophomore in high school." Not sure if I should hug her or shake her hand, instead I do nothing.

She claims the seat my mom just left. "Do you have a boyfriend?"

Her casual tone doesn't match how deep the question digs into my private life. I stare at her. Maybe the stress of what happened to her brother—my grandfather!—is affecting her. I lock my hands on my lap. "I don't get the question."

14

But her gaze is steady.

"InshaALLAH—which means God willing—when he recovers, my brother Tariq is going to get to know you. He's a deeply religious man, and he'll want to make sure his only grandchild understands the faith your mom ran away from."

The throbbing across my forehead tries to pull my eyes shut. "What are you saying?"

"Leena, your grandfather and I are all the family left on your maternal side. We're Muslims. Your mom was raised as one." Her sly smile comes out of nowhere. "It would bring my ailing brother so much peace to introduce you to our way of life. One day you might decide to accept Islam."

My brain hurts.

Raised as a Muslim? Ma doesn't fit the submissive stereotype I've seen in the media. Neither, it seems, does Aunt Samira.

"I'm just wondering how much freedom you've been given." She rests her hand on my shoulder for a quick second. Her tone has softened, but I'm not impressed.

I don't know what this woman, whoever the hell she is, wants from me. It's too much to digest. Why does someone I've known for five minutes think they can change me?

I've always wanted it to be more than me and my mom. Always.

But now I have an aunt, who's part of a religion I know almost nothing about, so my life feels nauseatingly different.

Ignoring a woman I just found out is a close relative is almost impossible, but I try. After I text DeeDee and cancel our plans, every person who comes into the ER waiting room gets my undivided attention. A guy dressed in a plaid jacket, dirty jeans, and work boots takes my glances as an invitation to wink. I turn away, my cheeks on fire.

"Leena, I'm heading to the gift shop. Are you hungry? Thirsty? InshaALLAH, I'm getting myself something to drink. Do you want anything?"

A loud rumble comes from my stomach. Maybe she'll ignore that.

After a quick look around the room, Samira leans close to me. "Maybe you shouldn't stay here by yourself. Just text your mom and let her know we went to get some snacks. We can bring something back for her."

"Thanks...but I want to be here when my mom comes out." Gifting her half a smile is all I can do. "If you can bring back two ginger ales, that'd be great."

Samira shrugs and walks away.

My phone pings with new notifications, and I lose myself in technology.

"Leena." My mom approaches me, her feet shuffling along the linoleum floor. Our eyes meet, and her sadness looks back at me.

Scrambling to my feet, I tuck my phone in my back pocket. "Yes, Ma?"

She wraps her arm around my shoulders. "Are you okay? I've been gone awhile." She glances around the waiting room. "Where's Samira? I can't believe she left you here all alone."

Not her too. I blow out a gush of air. "I'm fine. How's your dad?"

Her running her hands down the sides of her dress over and over again tells me everything I need to know. "He's stable."

Looking past my mom, I see Samira striding over. I count twelve steps until she reaches us. "How is he? What are these doctors doing for him? InshaALLAH, they reached his cardiologist!"

"Samira, calm down. He's well cared for." My mom's usually sweet tone is laced with annoyance. "The nurse gave him some medicine to prevent blood clots. They're waiting to move him into a room."

Samira hands her a bottle of ginger ale.

The two of them eye each other without saying a word.

"Thanks," I whisper, as she turns to hand one to me. The awkwardness is unbearable.

After taking a sip, my mom announces, "I'm taking Leena home."

My aunt's face twists. "You should stay until Tariq's settled. Is it too much to ask, Asiyah? He is your father. Maybe after all these years, it's easy to forget."

Me staring at the floor doesn't help dispel the tension surrounding the three of us. My stomach aches.

"Look, Samira..." my mom starts. "I don't need the guilt trip. Parking my daughter here for hours isn't an option. We're going, but I'll be back tomorrow. Text me his room number once you know it."

Her clipped words leave my aunt's mouth open. Mine too.

"Let's go, Leena."

I'm out of the seat in two seconds. Meeting my aunt's gaze one last time, I mumble, "Thanks for the drink. Nice to meet you."

After walking through the parking lot, we slide into my mom's Subaru. We're halfway home before she speaks up.

"I know there's a lot you don't understand, but we can talk tomorrow. Today has been a *day*—for both of us."

A thousand percent true.

"We didn't have to leave," I whisper. "If you wanted to stay longer, we could've. You know I have books on my phone—I'm okay with whatever." Both my voice and my body shake.

She doesn't answer.

If we're really going home...then fingers crossed, my mom will answer my questions tonight. As long as I don't chicken out—like most times. After a few minutes picking at my stubby fingernails, I get my nerve up.

"What's up with you and Samira?" I swallow. "Did she do something to you sixteen years ago to make you talk to her like that?"

"*Look*, Leena." My mom slams on the brakes, waiting for a light. "My aunt and I have always had our issues. You don't get it. You have no idea what she's like. I only brought you to the hospital in the first place because I thought your grandfather was about to pass."

My heart's hammering. "She bought us drinks, then offered to feed me.... Maybe she's not that bad *now*."

"How can you say that?" She pulls into our driveway, then faces me. "One meeting, and now you're an expert about all things Samira Stewart? You don't know her *or* my father."

Thoughts race through my brain. All the stuff I missed out on. Poor little Leena crying herself to sleep because she missed out on the Father-Daughter Dance, because she never attended Donuts with Dads at school. A grandfather to step in would've been great.

What if he's nice? What if he even loves me?

"Ma... You're right about one thing. I'm trying to understand, but those two people are strangers to me—all thanks to *you*." I rush out of the car and into the house before she gets from behind the steering wheel.

A million different feelings are hitting me all at the same time.

After grabbing a chewy granola bar from the daycare stash in the kitchen, I speed-walk into my room.

Slamming the door shut gives me a weird satisfaction.

Minutes later, my snack is history. Without changing out of my clothes, I curl up on my bed and wait for sleep to comfort me.

CHAPTER
THREE

November

"Leena, wake up."

I snuggle with the blanket I don't remember putting over me.

"Leena." Mom raps on my now-open bedroom door. "Samira just texted me my dad's room number. You can come with me, if you want. We'll stop at Satellite first...and talk."

After I sit up, our gazes meet for a nanosecond. "Give me fifteen minutes."

With three minutes to spare, I am showered, dressed, and in the car. Once we park outside our favorite coffee spot, I follow her inside.

We order and sit. I have a steaming mug of hot cocoa in front of me before she opens up.

"Leena, I'm sorry to have kept so much from you," she begins, "but my life went to hell after my mom died. Within a month, your great-aunt Samira came to live with us. My dad found comfort in the faith, while I didn't....Yes, I was born Muslim, but my mom was my everything. She filled our lives with joy, and when she was alive, our family was happy."

I gasp watching a tear run down her cheek. "Ma, what happened to make you run away?" I whisper, leaning in.

"*Damn.*" Her voice is a sliver of its normal volume. "When I was in middle school, my mom put me in martial arts. At first, it was just to keep healthy, but after six months I was hooked on tae kwon do." A smile spreads over her face. "Four years later, I was good. Really good. My sabeomnim told me the Olympic team could be in my future. But right before my black belt testing, Mom died, and Dad decided it wasn't okay for me to continue to train with teenage boys and men."

I don't get it. "Why?"

She sighs. "My dad believes once boys and girls hit puberty, they shouldn't do stuff together more than is absolutely necessary."

A terrible thought enters my brain.

"Does that mean...You got pregnant before you were married, right? Did your father...throw you out?"

"My experience with my dad is mine. I don't have any regrets, and you shouldn't feel bad about yourself now."

Too late.

With so many unanswered questions, I don't know what to think.

By the time we get to Presbyterian, my self-image is on life support.

My mom steps out of the car, waiting for me to stand beside her. "Be careful, daughter. My dad and aunt always have ulterior motives. You know who you are. Don't let them make you change yourself, to make up for how I removed myself from their control."

I'm chewing on my bottom lip and trying to ignore the flips inside my stomach. Good thing I didn't tell her about any of Aunt Samira's comments yesterday. She'd lose it.

As we're striding into the main lobby, heading towards the elevators, my uncertainty soars along with my pulse. What if my grandfather takes one look at me and never wants to see me again?

What if I symbolize the loss of his only child?

What if he blames *me* for the breakup of his family?

After a quick elevator ride, we arrive at the cardiac care unit. Its waiting room is all faded grey carpet and worn fabric chairs. Doesn't exactly give off a cheery, everything-is-going-to-be-okay vibe.

"Leena, wait for me here. Let me see if my dad is up and ready for visitors." Mom heads off.

I plunk myself down in a chair. Staring out the windows gives me a view of the traffic on Unser Boulevard.

Going over everything Mom shared with me, a heaviness in my stomach weighs me down. I've always wanted a bigger family, but now they might not want me because I'm the result of a mistake—or a sin. I don't know enough about Islam to know if there's a difference.

I finish fifteen minutes of IG scrolling before my mom returns.

"Are you ready?" she asks.

The pungent smell of disinfectant fills my nostrils as we walk down the hallway. Right outside room 405, the air stills as my mom pushes on the door and we step inside.

I expect a sickly old man. Instead, my grandfather is sitting up, his posture perfectly straight, his cheekbones strong. His light blue gown is dingy against his copper-brown skin. He puts down his newspaper and greets me with a huge smile.

"Hello, Leena. You are so lovely—like your mom when she was a teenager." The gleam in his gaze and the warmth in his voice soothe my nerves.

"Hi. Thanks." Trying to remember my manners, I ask, "How are you feeling today?"

"I feel better than yesterday, Alhamdulillah."

Before I can ask, my mom explains: "It means praise be to God."

"I'm glad you haven't forgotten *everything* from your childhood, Asiyah." My grandfather points to the two chairs in his private room. "Come sit down and keep me company."

I only move once my mom does. Thankfully, she sits closest to him.

He focuses on me. "It's nice to finally meet, young lady. Tell me something about you."

As I glance around the room, with its sterile white walls and blinking machines, my voice wavers. "I...I'm sixteen and a high school sophomore. Other than working at Mom's daycare and hanging out with my best friend, Deidre, my life is pretty boring."

Now he's frowning. "Nonsense. You're a Stewart, Leena, and we're ambitious. Your mom was always a top student. What are your plans after high school?"

Not him too. My mom is constantly pushing me to work to my potential at school when all I want to do is spend every waking moment lost in a book. "Moving in with my best friend. Probably taking a couple of classes at CNM. I'll figure out what interests me then." Not very concrete, but at least it's something.

A frown wrinkles his forehead. "A community college isn't good enough. You need to aim higher, Leena." Next, he takes aim at my mom. "Asiyah, don't you agree?"

"*Dad*," she starts, with her hands clenched in her lap. "My daughter needs to find what she's passionate about and what will make her happy—sometimes that doesn't mean a college degree."

Their stare-off makes me squirm in my seat.

"Anyway, we didn't come today to stress you out. You should rest." My mom inches closer to the bed. "Do you need something to drink? More water maybe?"

The corners of his mouth inch into a smile. "That would be nice, thank you."

After grabbing his plastic water pitcher, she heads out of the room.

"Now, Leena, it was nice of you to be here, but I'd really like us to spend time together once I'm home." His gentle gaze warms my heart. "Would you like that?"

His offer is something I've dreamed about since elementary school.

Family. People who love and support you. People who are with you from the cradle to the grave. People you come from, who carry your history with them. Relationships that weather any storm. Hands that link around you, protecting you.

But my uncertainty wins out. "Maybe." What would Mom say?

My grandfather hands me the sports section and a pen. "Write your phone number here and I'll text you so you have mine too."

After a moment of thought, I scribble down the information and hand it back to him.

"Thank you, Leena. You've made this old man incredibly happy."

I glance at the door. "In a few weeks, when school's out for Christmas, my schedule will be...more open. I'll talk to Mom about visiting you."

The door creaks open, so I close my mouth.

26

Having to bring this up to my mom, knowing there's been no communication between these three adults for all sixteen years of my life, has my stomach rock hard.

≈

It's the Sunday before Thanksgiving, and I'm driving myself crazy. The few daycare kids scheduled to be here today canceled—so right now is, theoretically, the perfect time to mention my grandfather's offer to my mom. If only I had the nerve.

"You want cereal or a Pop-Tart, Leena?"

Our breakfast offerings aren't the healthiest, but neither of us knows much about cooking. Taste and convenience win out every time in this house. We like it that way.

"I'll have cereal." Halfway through my second bowl, a familiar car horn erupts from the driveway. Deidre. I push my chair back, but my mom beats me to the front door.

Once Deidre is inside and sitting in the chair next to me, she asks the most direct question imaginable. "How was meeting your grandfather for the first time?"

Avoiding tough subjects isn't her style.

She scans our faces, then offers, "Sorry—taboo subject?"

Mom gives her a warm smile. "Deidre, you know there is no such thing in my house. I'm not that kind of parent."

Now they're both staring at me.

DeeDee knows me too well, so it's pointless for me to lie. I'll have to be honest. "My aunt Samira is nosy...but not terrible. She bought me something to drink, anyway." I take a swig of the juice pouch I swiped from the daycare stash. "My grandfather is nothing like I expected. He's not all wrinkled and frail. He actually looked really tall."

Mom's sudden laugh doesn't help my nervousness at all. "He is. My father should be able to go home tomorrow or the next day," she tells both of us. "Anything after that, I'm not sure."

Before I can open my mouth, she transfers her coffee into a to-go tumbler. "All right, chickadees, I have a couple of errands to run. There's your list of cleaning tasks." She points to a piece of paper on the fridge, then grabs her purse and coat off the couch. "I need everything finished today. After that, you two have a free afternoon."

I chickened out again. I didn't tell her about what my grandfather said.

Maybe later.

At least DeeDee is still here.

"Guess what? Tariq asked if we could get together at his house after he's released from the hospital." Sneaking a glance at my bestie, I ask, "Do you think I should?"

Her hard stare hints at her answer. "Are you sure this is something you want to do? What did your mom say?"

"Don't know, since I haven't told her."

"Leena!" DeeDee nudges me with her elbow. "You're keeping secrets from her? Are you ready to accept the consequences? These people—there's gotta be a reason your mom cut them off."

Ignoring that is easier than answering. "It's been almost *two decades* since my mom has been around Tariq *or* Samira. People change." I cross my arms over my chest. "Unless you're saying you don't think they'll like me? What's wrong with me?"

"Chill. That's not what I'm saying."

All I can hear at this very second is my inner self-doubt: What if my grandfather just wants to get to know me to ease the guilt of avoiding his own daughter for sixteen years? The rebellious daughter who had me at seventeen after running away from home.

Why would he care about *me*?

Pressing my palms against my thighs helps my overthinking not consume my brain.

"*Leeennnaaa!*" DeeDee yells into my ear.

I scoot my chair away from her, giving her my best WTF face. "Okay, definitely heard you. Something you want to say?"

"I get it. Since forever, you've wanted to find family beyond your mom...but you need to listen to her on this one. She grew up with them." Putting salt in the wound, she adds, "You're lucky to have her. Your life could be so much worse."

My best friend is the expert on that.

Her parents died six years ago in a small-plane crash caused by a drunk pilot. The only person available to raise her was her maternal grandmother, Lily. Yes, Lily stepped up, and yes, she used the settlement money to buy the nice three-bedroom house they live in, but the woman barely keeps food in the fridge. DeeDee never "fit her lifestyle" either, and she reminds DeeDee of this all the time. My ride-or-die's bedroom used to be a guest space, and Lily still complains about "losing" it. With my and my mom's help, DeeDee now has a secondhand double bed, not a twin. My mom tries to give DeeDee the mothering her own grandmother refuses to do.

But because of that, DeeDee, of all people, should get my not-so-secret obsession with finding my extended family. I love her like a sister, but I want *more*.

I leave the table and grab the to-do list off the fridge. Talking and working don't have to go together.

An hour passes in silence. We clean nonstop.

But eventually I'm done biting my tongue. "It's messed up how much support I'm *not* getting from you."

DeeDee finishes mopping the kitchen floor, then meets my stare. "You know me, L. I always tell you the truth. If I can't be honest with my best friend, who can I be honest with?" She steps out towards me. "I don't want you to forget how great you have it here."

A light goes off in my brain. "Wait. Did you have another argument with Lily?"

30

Stuffing her hands in the back pockets of her jeans, DeeDee nods.

I should've known.

≈

"What is her problem this time?" I plop down into a chair.

"The usual. The house isn't neat enough. I work harder here than I do where I sleep at night, et cetera."

My fingers drum on the dining table in front of me. "That's ridiculous. When is the last time she touched the vacuum cleaner?" Red-hot anger rises inside of me. "I bet she still doesn't put her dirty dishes in the dishwasher."

DeeDee sits beside me. "Girl, it's so stupid. How hard is it to pick up your damn plate and at least put it in the sink?" A sly smile slides onto her face. "You know she'd curse us out if she knew we talked about her."

I snap my fingers in the air. "Make sure you don't let it slip."

"You know I barely say anything when I'm there," she says. "My life is easier that way. Let's get some boba tea. You down?"

≈

That evening, wrapped in a blanket and reading my newest YA fantasy (a find from our local used bookstore), I'm still feeling unsettled. I finish the last sentence on my page and put the book down.

I have to follow what my heart's telling me. And it's telling me to connect with my grandfather. *As long as I do what feels right, there's nothing to worry about.*

If I keep saying that, the universe might make it true.

Without knocking, my mom steps into my room. "Leena, do you have a minute?"

The serious frown on her face speeds up my heart rate. I sit up and brace myself against the wall. "Is this about our family?"

"Look..." She moves her hands to her hips. "Them wanting to spend time with you is a given, and whether you do or not is your decision. But I don't want you to expect me to do the same. We have history. Any relationship you have with them won't change anything for me."

I grab my pillow and hold on tight. "Samira reached out to you first. That's a sign she wants to re-establish a relationship, right?" *And get to know me too.* "Would it really be that bad?"

She plants herself in my desk chair. "For me, yes...but I've been thinking, and I recognize that you shouldn't reject them because of me. I'm not going to forbid you from talking to them. That would be more like my Aunt Samira's way of thinking—she's always been a spiteful—"

"Ma, really?" She's killing my dream. I refuse to believe my aunt is that bad. "What happened to make you talk about her like that?"

"Going deeper into that with you, right now, isn't something I'm doing tonight." She's staring through my small bedroom window, her hands pressed flat on her lap. "Do what you want, Leena. Don't complain to me when it all goes wrong."

My doubts double as she strides out of my room.

I'm halfway off my bed to follow her when my phone rings. It's a local number. I don't recognize it but answer anyway. "Hello?"

"Salaam, Leena! This is Tariq, your grandfather. How are you today?"

His kind voice is such a relief after my mom's sharp words. I'm thrilled to hear from him. "I'm okay. But you're the one who just had a heart attack! How are *you* feeling?"

"Alhamdulillah, I feel better today. Thank you for asking. Are you busy?"

After shaking my head (like he can see me...), I say, "No, not really. What does 'Alhum...alhumdallah' mean again?"

"It means praise be to God. I'm not surprised your mom hasn't shared those words with you."

There's a sadness in his voice, so sincere it almost snatches away my breath. He's *got* to still care about my mom.

"Has your mother told you anything about the faith she was born into?"

"No. I'm sorry." I have not a clue if my answer will offend him. He's still mostly a stranger. "She never mentioned it once."

His sigh rings in my ears.

33

"Why didn't you ever try to contact her? She's your only child, right?" Wrapping myself tighter in my blanket, I take it to a deeper level. "Weren't you ever curious about me?"

I freeze my entire body until he answers.

"Leena, my own daughter believed I was a monster. That I *wanted* her gone. Nothing could have been further from the truth! But after the police and the private investigator I hired didn't find anything, I gave up. She would have been an adult by then—eighteen. It may seem silly to you, but I put my faith in ALLAH and prayed Asiyah would be safe. Maybe it was a terrible decision...but she was still hurt from losing her mom and wanted to rebel against everything in our life. She clearly didn't want me to find her."

His calm voice doesn't fool me. My grandfather *does* care about my mom. I know he does. I can tell.

"But we can talk about that more after we've gotten to know each other. How about it?"

I bite my bottom lip while my brain works. "I...Yes. Sure."

"Alhamdulillah. How about you come over to my house soon? As long as you're not busy. I'll ask Samira if she can arrange transportation to Santa Fe if you agree. We'll have a late dinner."

Two opposing realities pull at me. I don't want my mom to be pissed, but there is *no way* I can give up this chance—a chance I've wanted forever.

"Could we meet after my finals? I'll have a ton of free time then! It has to be after four on the days the daycare is open. I'll text you our address."

"Great. InshaALLAH, we'll see each other soon. As-salaamu alaykum."

"It was nice speaking to you! Goodbye!" I end the call, then throw myself back and count the popcorn on my ceiling. Even that doesn't calm me down.

Finding a way to tell Mom about this invitation might be the hardest thing I've ever had to do.

CHAPTER
FOUR

December

It should be illegal for sixteen-year-olds to have to be awake and functional before 7 a.m.

But even if it were, my mom would still expect me to be sitting at our table bright and early, slouched over a bowl of soggy cereal. (Never mind that I suffered through all my finals yesterday.)

"Are you sure you don't want some coffee?" She points to the machine on the kitchen counter. "Instant works just as well as the fancy stuff."

I wave away her suggestion. "Nothing can wake me up right now."

Wrong choice. Hours later, surrounded by toddler-created block towers, I'm exhausted. Every crayon and piece of construction paper they yanked from our craft box is scattered throughout the house. *Get to work*, I tell myself, *or this mess will never be cleaned up.* The daily reclaiming of our house begins shortly after, and by the time the rooms are straightened up, with all toys in their places, I am dead.

From the living room, I watch DeeDee wipe down the kitchen counters. The loud hum of the dishwasher numbs me.

Mom joins me on the couch. The stink of mushed peas surrounds me.

"Yuck, Mom...Did you get *any* of the baby food in Chloe's mouth?"

She glances down at the green stains decorating her work shirt. "I was dirtier when you were an infant. Spitting out food was your favorite thing to do." Her smile can't hide the tiredness behind her eyes. "Leena, when were you going to tell me about my dad's invitation? I've waited, but you haven't brought it up. Samira let me know over a week ago."

My palms dampen. An itch tickles my throat.

"I'm sorry," I manage. "I talked to Tariq—I mean, my grandfather—before Thanksgiving, that's true, but nothing was decided. We just set a date last week..."

Crossing my fingers under my throw blanket probably won't help, but I do it anyway.

It doesn't help.

Mom's normally happy smile isn't there. Flat, pressed-together lips are what I get. "In the future, don't hide your plans with your grandfather. You already know how I feel about this, anyway." She's off the couch the very next second.

I blurt out, "You're not mad, are you?"

She locks her gaze to mine. "I gave you my permission to see them. At sixteen, you are allowed to make mistakes, but make sure you learn from them." With that gem of parental advice, she heads into her bedroom.

It's the door slam that really shakes my confidence.

I pull my legs onto the sofa and stare at the plain grey carpet. That didn't feel great. Granted...I should have told her...but I *knew* she would hate it, and she did.

"Want to know my opinion?" DeeDee's asking from the kitchen entryway, a red-and-white towel in her hands.

"When has that mattered?" I throw back at her, nervousness controlling my words. "You've never been too shy to share."

She dries her hands, then drops the kitchen towel onto the table, before coming over and claiming the opposite end of our couch. "Your hostility is off the charts. Not cool." DeeDee gives me her best *I'm-serious, listen-to-me-just-once* face. "Are you really willing to damage the relationship between you and your mom for people you don't even know?"

"But that's the thing, DeeDee." Wild, resentful thoughts swirl around in my head. "This isn't about *her*—it's for *me*. It's about something she kept from me, knowing I've always wished for it. Needed it." My grief for what I've never had mixes with my anger, but crying isn't an option. "I want to know my family. Can't you understand?"

A couple seconds later, she's right next to me. "Leena, I *do* support you...but just don't get too attached to them too soon."

I'm not sure if that clarification really makes things any better. "Okay."

DeeDee glances at her phone. "I gotta go. Lily wants me to pick up fried chicken on the way home, and my grandmother always gets what she wants. We good?"

"You know it." A small disagreement will never break our bond. I won't let it.

"See you tomorrow." With that, she grabs her keys and leaves.

I was already nervous about visiting my grandfather. Now, after these unenthusiastic, far-too-honest conversations, I'm terrified. Fingers crossed, everything will be great—and that my mom will go with me to see him, eventually.

Aren't we all supposed to dream big?

Well, universe, get to work for me.

I need you.

≈

Friday morning, two minutes before my alarm is set to go off, I get a new text notification.

> As-salaamu alaykum, Leena. InshaALLAH, I'll be at the South Capitol stop at 5:45 p.m. to pick you up. I'll drive you home later. Samira.

Shit. I thought the plan was that she'd pick me up here. Instead, I have to take the train to Sante Fe!

It's fine. Everything's fine. I'll make it work.

Miscommunications happen all the time, right?

After typing a fast "See you later," I throw on my work polo and a pair of jeans, race to wash my face and brush my teeth, and finally pull my thick shoulder-length hair back with a scrunchie. The daycare opens soon.

"Leena, I hope you're up. Breakfast is ready!" My mom's booming voice finds me in front of the bathroom mirror.

I can do this. I can face her, even though I know she doesn't want me to do this. What's the worst that can happen?

With each step I take towards the kitchen, my heart thumps harder in my chest. But when I reach it, instead of our regular instant foods, I find a home-cooked plate of scrambled eggs, turkey bacon, and toast smothered with strawberry jam.

My stomach growls.

"What's all this?" I ask, licking my lips. "Who are you and what have you done with my mother?"

Hands on her ample hips, Mom frowns. "Don't look so surprised. I've made these kinds of foods before. You've never gone hungry, have you?"

"No. Thanks for this. Everything smells great." After taking a bite of turkey bacon, I pause and ask, "Are you really allergic to pork, or is it because of growing up Muslim that you don't eat it?"

"Once I didn't live with my dad, I tried regular bacon, but I didn't like it. The allergy thing was easier to explain to people."

Since when is your own daughter "people"?

Mom joins me at the only adult-sized table in the house. "Do you and Deidre have plans tonight? If not, I thought you might want to go with me to the educational store and check out their clearance section?"

I force the lump down in my throat. "Sounds great but I already agreed to visit my grandfather tonight. I'm taking the train up and Samira is bringing me back. Why don't you ask DeeDee to go with you? She loves a good sale."

Her hopeful smile drops away. "Oh, okay," and then she gets up.

I ask her, "Aren't you going to eat something?"

"I already did." Seconds later, she's gone and I'm alone.

≈

DeeDee shows up to work an hour late, but my mom barely blinks at that. Me, though—I leave a washable marker out and one of the preschoolers draws a mustache on himself, and she gives me laundry duty.

"Leena, can you gather the blankets from the playpens and the sheet from the crib? Everything is dirty and needs to be washed."

I get that she's pissed, but does she have to give me the grunt work?

By three-thirty, all the daycare kids have been picked up, my feet and lower back ache, and my mom heads into her room and closes the door.

I could be wrong...but it's like she doesn't want to see me leave to visit her childhood home.

Deidre and I recover stretched out on the couch.

Finally, she blurts out, "So...you're really doing this. Damn." She inches closer to me, then asks, "Are you nervous?"

I nod. "Scared to death."

She reaches over and pinches my forearm. "Your aunt is coming here?"

"Well...no." I clear my throat. "I need you to drop me off at the Montaño Rail Runner station. The northbound train leaves at four-thirty."

"Sure."

"What are you doing tonight?"

DeeDee holds out her hands to me, chipped polish on full display. "Maybe I'll paint my nails and veg out with Netflix."

"What about dinner?"

"You sound more like your mom every day," she teases. "Dinner is my problem."

I go into the kitchen and take out a single-serve frozen dinner from the freezer. After tucking it in a plastic grocery bag, I hand it to DeeDee.

"Not anymore. I got you."

She takes a peek inside. "You're sharing one of your favorite veggie lasagnas. I'm impressed."

"Give me ten minutes to change."

42

Since the City Different is colder than here in Albuquerque, my outfit is a chunky green turtleneck sweater and black jeans. Not sure if these clothes are appropriate to wear when visiting your newly discovered Muslim grandfather, I touch my toes to make sure the jeans aren't *too* tight. Finally, I grab my fleece-lined jean jacket.

DeeDee rises off the sofa when I return. "I expect to hear from you when you get home from your visit. Do *not* leave me hanging, because I *will* worry. I swear, if you don't..."

Holding up my hand, I promise, "On the life of my library card, you will get a text later with every detail of what happened." I step into my chunky black boots, then yell, "Ma, we're leaving!"

My mom flings open her bedroom door. "Be careful. Text me if...anything happens."

We're out the door five seconds later.

DeeDee is super quiet the entire ride. As soon as we get to the station, she parks. "Stay safe. I don't want this to be the last time I ever see you. Stay away from any overly friendly dudes. And run if your relations start acting weird."

My half smile is all I can manage. "I'll share my location when I get there. It should be fine."

I'm not sure if tonight is really going to work, but I'm going to Tariq's house anyway. Maybe it will be perfect! (But probably not, because I exist in the sucky real world.)

All I can do is hope.

CHAPTER
FIVE

December

A loud announcement ushers passengers in as I board the Rail Runner: "Welcome aboard! If you're joining us going northbound, please keep your feet off the seat...."

I snag a red pleather seat at a table for four, crossing my fingers I don't have to share. And then we're moving. Once I show my e-ticket to a smiling grey-haired conductor, no one else talks to me. Good thing, because no matter how much I will them still, my legs shake. It doesn't help that the ride rocks me from side to side.

Outside, the only thing to look at are fields of brown grass, so my phone is the better alternative. After fifty minutes of scrolling bookstagram, I check the electronic sign. Three more stops until mine.

> Me: DeeDee, maybe coming was wrong.
> HUGE mistake???

> DeeDee: Girlie, don't flake out now

I try to slow my breathing. We're almost there.

> Samira: InshaALLAH, five minutes away.

"Next, South Capitol station."

Lingering doubts challenge me. I talk myself out of listening to them.

We arrive. Shakily, I stand and exit the car. The bitter chill of today's Santa Fe wind hits me right in the face as I step onto the open-air station. (You'd think the capital city of the state would have a stop with four walls.) I button up my jean jacket and pull my gloves on.

I've only been in the evening air for a few minutes when a dark grey Range Rover pulls up into the closest parking space. My aunt does not step out. Instead, a loud honk is all I get.

I race over to the door and fling myself into the passenger seat.

"Hello, Leena," Aunt Samira says. Her flat words lack any emotion.

"Hi!" I stumble around in my brain, figuring out what to say next. "Wha... what should I call you?"

"Aunt Samira is fine." She backs the car up. "How was your trip?"

"Fine." My hands dampen inside my gloves. "It was kind of bumpy."

The expensive car—with its two-tone seats and fancy paneling—feels a little bit like a beautiful prison; the

45

atmosphere is so awkward. With nothing else to say, my focus shifts to the narrow street we're driving on. The dusting of snow isn't slowing traffic down. Almost every house we pass is adobe—just like red and green chili—as a New Mexican, I'm used to it, but it looks extra beautiful in winter weather.

"Do you live in a house or an apartment?" Samira asks coolly.

"A house—we've been there since I was one."

She checks her rearview mirror, then glances at my face. "Is it just the two of you?"

"Yeah, I've never lived with anyone else."

Wow! What she's really asking: *Is your mother exposing you to men—to her boyfriends? Is she irresponsible?* A wave of anger rises inside my gut.

"That's good, at least."

"Are you upset that I'm here?" I blurt out.

My newfound great-aunt frowns. "Not unless you pull the same nonsense Asiyah did. My brother has been through *enough*. I won't stand for him to be put under more stress because of family issues."

Wow.

That's what she thinks of me and my mom. A source of stress: one new, one old.

Samira stays quiet after that, and I do too. I hope it's not too much longer to the house she shares with her brother, my grandfather.

Am I having fun yet?

We turn into a gated community: LAS CAMPANAS is what the sign reads. The SUV drives along a winding street dotted with snow-capped trees for, like, ever. Every house we pass has beautiful Christmas lights, and a few have a row of luminarias decorating the edges of their roofs. They're all so far apart I don't think the neighbors know each other.

As we finally pull into a circular driveway, my mouth drops open. "How many people live here?"

"Just me and Tariq," Samira says, her bland tone hitting me the wrong way. "Our housekeeper works five days a week but doesn't live with us."

It's an enormous house, and its immaculate, xeriscaped front lawn doesn't have a stone out of place. I follow Samira out of the car to the massive, dark wood front door.

"Do you . . . have a job?"

Aunt Samira whips around, her eyebrows bunching together.

I flinch. "Sorry. That sounded better in my head."

The door opens. I take my first steps into the foyer and freeze. It looks like marble.

"You can put your shoes here and hang your coat up in the closet right there."

I follow her directions, stashing my jean jacket and my boots—their dirty exterior doesn't match this place.

"Follow me, Leena." Samira strides down the right hallway, pointing to things along the way. "That's the downstairs half bath."

We pass through an immense living room, all dark wood and rich brown leather couches and light cream walls. The super high ceilings taper to three skylights. I catch a glimpse of a huge kitchen counter the next room over too (one too big for my entire house).

"Wow!" My feet stick as I try to take all of this in. Not a single item is out of place—it's like they live in a model home.

"Come. The last door on the right is Tariq's office. That's our destination."

My mouth's dry, but my forehead's damp. I'm a mess. Before I know it, we reach *the* door.

Samira knocks. "As-salaamu alaykum. You have a visitor."

"Wa alaykum as salaam, come in."

Aunt Samira opens the door and strides inside. Me, on the other hand...all I can manage is to tiptoe after her.

My gaze takes in the large L-shaped desk; the wooden filing cabinets; the bookshelves that cover an entire wall. I don't miss the two monitors or the silver laptop either. My grandfather sits in a huge brown leather chair. Beside him, a full plate of fruit and a big black mug sit undisturbed.

"Salaam, Leena, how are you today?" His wide smile is contagious. "You've made this old man happy. Please, sit here with me," he says, pointing to the seat closest to his chair.

Sitting with a super straight spine, I clasp my hands together in my lap. "Wow. This office is bigger than my bedroom."

He smiles even harder. "InshaALLAH, you can visit as much as you want. One day, my daughter will be okay with you spending the night, I'm sure. We have two spare bedrooms."

Only two? I don't believe it.

The hope I spot on his face is sweet, but getting Mom to agree to something like that is an uphill battle I'm not ready to fight. His facial expression is burned in my memory, though.

"I would like that."

"Leena, are you hungry? My sister here cleaned out all my favorite unhealthy snacks, but we've got lots of fruit. Right, Samira?"

I kinda forgot my aunt—she hasn't said a single word. She's simply standing behind me, arms crossed over her chest. "Tariq, you haven't touched your tea or anything else I brought you! Leena, what would you like? Maybe if you eat something, your grandfather will too."

Her harsh words are wrapped in concern. She really does love her brother.

I can do my part.

"Sure, do you have herbal tea? If not, water is fine." Looking at Tariq's untouched plate of grapes, I add, "Grapes would be great, but no kiwi, please—it's not my favorite."

Samira chuckles. "She is definitely a Stewart. Has the same taste buds as you, Tariq. Here, I'll heat this up again," she says, lifting his full mug and vanishing.

49

There's a long moment. Curiosity gets the best of me, so I ask, "What do you do?"

My grandfather pops a green grape in his mouth. Once he's done chewing, he tells me, "I own some commercial real estate and a couple of businesses. There's an Islamic bookstore, a barbershop, and a hair salon in the strip mall next to the biggest masjid in Albuquerque."

"Can anyone go into those places, or is it just for Muslims?" His smile hasn't gone anywhere, so maybe my question isn't rude. If he *does* get angry, all this could be over before we really know each other. But I'm just so curious.

Aunt Samira is back with my grandfather's hot tea and a bottle of fancy French water. On her second trip, she sets down a plate of green and red grapes next to my water.

"Of course, they are open for all customers. The salon has private rooms, so Muslim women who wear hijab can take them off in private and still get their hair done." After a quick sip of tea, he continues. "It wouldn't be particularly good business sense to sell only to Muslims. I want to help my faith community, but my businesses welcome everyone."

"Makes sense."

His eyes brighten. "You should really think about studying entrepreneurship in college. We Stewarts have a knack for business."

He might be right. My mom has her home daycare, after all, and I can't remember her ever doing anything else.

But school and my lack of educational direction aren't something I really want to talk about. So I stay quiet, unsure of a polite way to deflect.

Tariq's smile disappears. "Your future is important and shouldn't be played around with."

A loud wind rustles the tall blue spruce outside the picture window. "It's Christmas break, and my grades are good... isn't it time for fun?" I dare to ask.

"It's not a choice. You can work and have fun, both," he reminds me. "Making a concrete plan for your final two years of high school will give you something to follow. Or do you think you can't improve your GPA?"

My heart's pounding. "My GPA isn't the best. Honestly... I've got no clue what I want to do after high school."

"I understand. Just promise me this: You will talk to one of the college counselors when school starts again." He eyes me with a wary look. "Can you do that?"

I barely glance at him before saying, "Sure." Time to change the subject. This is not going well. "So... why do so many Muslim women cover their hair? What's up with that?"

Before he can answer, my aunt speaks up. "Covering your hair is something most Muslims believe is a commandment from God." She points to her own loose-fitting pants and oversized blouse. "Also, not wearing form-fitting clothes and exposing too much skin allows Muslim women to be judged on their intellect and not their bodies."

I don't totally understand. "What about guys? Do they have to cover their hair?"

Samira's lips flatten and her eyes narrow.

My grandfather jumps in. "Ladies, before we get into every detail, I think it would be better if Leena had some understanding of our basic beliefs." He turns to his sister. "Samira, don't we have something on the pillars of Islam?"

While she's searching the massive bookcase, Tariq leans in, and whispers, "Sorry about Samira. My sister was really hurt when your mom ran away. She's always blamed herself." His voice shakes a little. "No one's to blame that we lost your grandmother—then your mom."

What if he needs this as much as I do? Fingers crossed.

"Here you go." Aunt Samira is back and hands me a pamphlet: *Five Pillars of Islam*. It isn't as interesting to me as the conversation she's interrupting.

I pretend to examine it, then polish off my grapes and drink some of my water. Who knew trying to impress your estranged grandfather would leave you parched?

Before I can ask him anything else, he yawns a couple of times. That's all Samira needs. "Okay, Leena, I think that's enough for today. My brother needs to rest." Her motherly tone is back. "He forgets he just got released from the hospital."

"Of course," I say, grabbing my stuff. "Thanks for inviting me, Tariq. Your house is beautiful."

"You are always welcome here, Leena."

I'm not ready for a hug, so I reach out my hand and we shake on it.

"Please don't be a stranger. I've already missed the first sixteen years. I'd hate to miss any more time with my only grandchild."

"I won't!" I promise, being rushed out by Aunt Samira.

After ushering me through the house all the way to the front door, she finally pauses and speaks. "Just so that we're clear: I hope you don't expect anything from my brother. Tariq is a sweetheart and would give you anything you asked for, so it's *my job* to make sure you and your mom don't take advantage of him."

Wait... *What?* Does she think I'm only getting to know my grandfather for *money* or something?

Her accusation hits me right in the heart.

Blowing out a breath, I slowly say, "You don't even know me, and you're already accusing me of something?" I clench my jaw to keep the tears from flowing. "I understand that you're protective of your brother, but us getting together was his idea—not mine."

Her frown softens slightly. "Didn't mean to offend you, but it had to be said."

This is going to be the longest sixty-minute drive back home in my life.

I try to think positive. Aunt Samira is just overprotective. She just doesn't understand me yet. And it's been her and her brother for so long. I'm a third wheel she never asked for.

"I'm glad my grandfather is so nice." My words come out at a snail's pace. "It makes it much easier to visit him again."

Unless he tells me to my face he doesn't want this relationship, I'm diving in with both feet. With or without Aunt Samira's approval.

CHAPTER
SIX

December

The house I step into is super quiet.

Every surface I see is clear of clutter and without a single crumb. Which means some serious stress-cleaning went on.

"Welcome home, daughter. So glad you remembered where you live." My mom strides past me and yanks open the dishwasher.

"Ma, let me..."

She turns, facing me. "How do you think I felt when I got a call from Samira telling me that you'd be home late?" The bright kitchen lights highlight her flared nostrils. "I'm pulling the mommy card. Let this be the *first and only time* you fail to tell me where you are. Knowing at all times is one of my responsibilities. *You* should have called."

Guilt should be eating me up. I could've texted. I *should've* been home earlier and helped her pick up the house. But to be 100 percent real, I've got nothing but warm feelings about the time I spent with my grandfather today.

"Ma, I'm sorry—I messed up." Even with the heater running, I'm shivering. "It'll never happen again."

"Fine," she says, a scowl still covering her face. "If you're hungry, there's some burritos in the freezer. Cooking isn't on my to-do list tonight."

"No, I'm good."

Me passing up one of my favorite foods doesn't get past my mom.

"Don't tell me," she chides. "Samira fed you something made from scratch and much healthier than anything *I* can give you."

"Ma, no, she didn't do—"

She turns and leaves. I count ten seconds until her door closes.

It hurts my heart. I blow out small breaths, tears pooling in my eyes. Sometimes life with my mom is hard, but…at least she's still here. Not like Deidre's parents. Not like my dad.

As I wipe at my lashes with the back of my hand, something clicks. Is it possible that my own mother *resents* me for this? For wanting to get to know people she ran away from?

Or…could my own mom be *jealous* that I'm getting to know her father and aunt?

Does she miss them?

My new relationship could show her what she can have if she tries.

The dread inside me turns to hope. Making it happen is my new mission.

CHAPTER
SEVEN

December

Tariq looks up from his keyboard, his eyebrows bunched together. "Is it safe to let Google store my passwords? What if I'm hacked?"

After a long sip of hot chocolate, I point at the task bar and say, "You'll be fine. See that shortcut? It's for your antivirus software. Next time, I can show you how to set up your password manager."

His silly grin warms me like our three hundred days of annual sunshine in New Mexico. "Thanks for helping an old man with this," he says, eyes gleaming. "For the last hour!"

Aunt Samira steps into his office, not stopping until she's right over my shoulder. "If you two are finished...I just took a mushroom-and-cheddar-cheese quiche out of the oven. InshaALLAH, lunch will be ready in ten minutes."

My grandfather turns off his new laptop without any help. A small win.

"Sounds delicious, Samira." He stands. "Leena, do you have time to eat with us?"

Looking at my phone, I nod. "My mom told me to be home by four o'clock since we have to get things ready for tomorrow's daycare kids."

"Perfect." He waves me in front of him. "Ladies first."

I follow Aunt Samira into their massive eat-in kitchen. It's not just homemade quiche on the peninsula: There's a platter of sliced tomatoes and cucumbers, a leafy green salad, and a plate of weird-looking burgers.

"Did you make all of this just for the three of us?" This is new for me. So much food. "And what kind of meat is that?"

Her smirk makes my self-confidence shrink. "I made everything except the veggie burgers. I wasn't sure how much healthy food you get at home. Your mom never wanted to learn how to cook."

I meet her gaze. "I don't starve."

"I hope today's last-minute invitation wasn't a problem with Asiyah." My grandfather's serious expression convinces me of his concern. "We weren't sure what the two of you usually do on Christmas day."

"Nothing." My pulse speeds up—I'm not really sure how to answer him. It feels like a loaded question. "When I was in elementary school, my mom would get a tiny fake tree. The daycare kids liked it." A quick memory of happier times flashes before me. "Now it's just a day off."

No need to mention we exchanged gifts this morning before Samira picked me up.

The visit is going well and my aunt doesn't need any more reason to judge my mom, her own niece.

Shifting the conversation, I ask, "So you're going vegan now?"

Tariq smiles. "No, but my doctor wants me to limit how much red meat I eat, and those veggie burgers aren't half-bad with some condiments." He sits on the closest bar stool, then pats the one next to his. "At least try one."

Between the hopeful look on his face and my empty stomach, I have no choice. "I can try anything once."

All it takes is a dollop of mayo and a slice of cheese to finish mine. Vegetables—other than carrots, like in carrot cake—aren't my favorite, but I manage. I also get down the salad without gagging.

Tariq and Samira are talking about an electrical problem in one of the businesses he owns, so I eat in silence. At home, my phone is always part of my meals, but I'm not sure if that would fly here, so it stays in my back pocket.

"So, I see your burger is gone. Did you like it?" His curiosity is cute.

"It was good." I nod. "You were right—the toppings made all the difference." I'm really enjoying the positive energy between the two of us. It releases some of the tightness in my shoulders. "And I also—"

"Are you sure you don't want a slice of quiche?" my aunt interrupts. "At least when you're here, I know you're eating healthy food."

My grandfather yawns twice.

"Are you okay?" I ask. He always seems so tired.

His big smile hasn't gone anywhere. "I'm fine."

That is all his sister needs to hear. "Leena, let me put this food away and I'll drive you home." Turning to face her brother, she says, "Tariq, you were in the hospital less than a month ago; you need to rest!"

"My little sister loves telling me what to do. I should've been nicer to her when we were kids." He winks at me as he stands. "You should take a plate with you, Leena. Please, we have plenty."

"Thanks, I think I will," I say, with the sides of my mouth inching up into a smile. "See you next weekend, right?"

"InshaALLAH, I'll be here." He turns to his sister. "Samira, can you tell her about the event next Saturday? I think it would be something she'd enjoy. Salaam, Leena."

"Goodbye."

With that, he heads down the hallway towards his master suite.

Not ten minutes later, we're driving, and my palms won't stop sweating. For some unknown reason, Aunt Samira hasn't said a word.

I guess it's up to me to start the conversation.

"So...Samira, what was Tariq talking about?" My curiosity is killing me. "Is the event next Saturday, like...a medical appointment or something?"

60

"No, it's nothing like that," she says without a drop of emotion. "Our masjid in Albuquerque is having a youth get-together next Saturday. Your grandfather thinks it's a safe way for you to meet some Muslim teenagers."

Too many thoughts creep in and fog up my brain. Masjid? "Is that a mosque? Is this going to be someone lecturing us?"

Her face lights up. Never seen that before. "No! There are arcade games, popcorn, and tons of chocolate chip cookies. It's for both boys and girls—but plenty of adult chaperones will be there to make sure there's no inappropriate behavior."

I don't ask what she considers inappropriate. We ride most of the rest of the way listening to each other breathe. Can't get into any trouble doing that.

I've never kissed anyone or been in a relationship—but Aunt Samira does *not* need to know that. As she takes the highway exit closest to us, I finally ask, "Can I even go? I mean...I'm not a Muslim."

"That doesn't matter," she tells me. "Your grandfather is well-known in our Islamic community, and inshaALLAH you'll be treated very well. It's a good alternative to other New Year's Eve things that would tempt our young people to do something forbidden, and it's open to any teenager in high school." The sides of her mouth actually curve into a small smile. "It would make Tariq very happy. Talk to Asiyah about it and let us know."

Samira switches on a PBS radio station, so I guess our conversation is over. By the time she pulls into our driveway, my eyes are half-closed. "Salaam, Leena."

I hop out of her car after a quick "Bye," my mind dwelling on her invitation. If it will make my grandfather happy, I'll go. Talking to my mom about it isn't going to be easy—I already expect a "Hell no"—but she always *says* there aren't any taboo topics, so finding the courage to bring it up will be on me.

≈

"Hey. You want to go somewhere with me next Saturday?" I ask DeeDee, biting my bottom lip.

She knows something is up immediately. "*Where*, exactly?"

"My grandfather invited me to a youth event at his mosque." I pause and check her face. Not catching a hint of frown, I continue. "It's some kind of open house thing. They've got chocolate and popcorn and carnival games. Apparently."

"Why are you going? You don't even like *the State Fair*."

She's right...but this is kinda different.

I shrug, not sure of the right words to say. "I'm curious about what my mom believed growing up. And...and what made her leave her family when she was only a little older than me."

"So you want me to go to hold your hand?"

At first, her sarcasm stings—but then I see the sly smile on her face. "You can't expect me to go alone, with only crabby Aunt Samira as my chaperone?"

"Chaperone? What do they think you'll do there?!" DeeDee chuckles. "I don't really understand, but okay, this could be interesting. Count me in."

"Yay!" Part one of Operation Attend the Party is complete. The next part—the conversation with my mother—won't be so easy.

"Leena, your mom just sent me a list of the things she wants us to do. You want the kitchen or the bathrooms?" DeeDee asks. "Also...hate to state the obvious...but telling *her* about Saturday won't be easy."

To give myself more time to figure out what to say, I jump up. "I call the bathrooms—be right back." I rush to the hallway closet and grab the bucket of cleaning products for my job. When I go back to the table, she's already in the kitchen, wearing a pair of Pepto-pink rubber gloves. "All right, serious answer: I was hoping my mom would let me go because I won't be by myself."

"Good plan—don't worry, I'll be with you for sure. But..." She points at me with her gloved hand. "If this thing is lame, you owe me big time."

I give her a quick hug. "Thank you!"

An hour later, I'm done with both bathrooms, while DeeDee, AKA the best employee, has cleaned every surface in the kitchen, vacuumed all the carpets, and organized the daycare toys. I'm a slacker compared to her. But at this very second, I don't care.

"You want to stay to eat?" I ask. "Not sure what we're having for dinner—probably something from the freezer."

"Can't. Got plans."

Wax must be clogging my ears. "You *do*? Why don't I know about them?" But then I catch worry in her eyes—something's off. "Is everything okay? Do you need—"

"I have a date."

DeeDee's confession rolls over me. I'm almost speechless. "What?" Pointing to the couch, I say, "Sit! Don't even *think* of leaving without an explanation."

She stays on her feet. "It's not a big deal! He's the grandson of one of Lily's friends." Fiddling with the string of her hoodie, she meets my gaze. "I planned to tell you...just... once it was over."

"But why did you say yes?" My hands wave around in the air. "You've never wanted a boyfriend."

She blows out a loud sigh. "Lily thinks you have to date. And that you have to date a ton of duds before you find 'the one.'"

"But why did you say yes to him *specifically*?"

She stares right at me, smiles, and admits, "He's really cute. But it was mostly so Lily would stop asking. She's always on my back about it. Like, always."

Knowing both of them, that makes total sense. "And where are you going with this cute boy whose name you haven't told me?" I fold my arms.

"Your pissed-off face is the best." She notices everything. "His name is Quan and we're meeting at the house. I gotta go home and change."

"The house? Your grandmother agreed to that?"

"It was her idea! She's cooking dinner for us, and I'm sure she's going to ask him a ton of embarrassing questions." She points at me. "After he sees me scarf down a double cheese-burger, we'll see if he's still interested."

"Promise you'll text me with every juicy detail," I insist.

She winks at me, then is gone.

Before I can make it into my bedroom and ask her to text me a picture of her outfit, the front door opens.

"Hey, Leena." My mom's greeting is nothing special, and her blank expression gives no hint as to her current mood. Should I risk asking her about the masjid, or not?

"H-hi," I stammer. "Doesn't it look great in here?"

"Smells clean." Mom stops at the edge of the kitchen. "Everything looks great. Where's Deidre?"

"She went home—something with her grandmother." I stretch the truth a little. "Can I talk to you?"

After setting down her coat, purse, and car keys, my mom claims the couch cushion farthest from mine. "Sure, what's up? Did you meet someone?"

"*No*, that's not it." I lick my lips and swallow my growing trepidation. "Tariq, um...invited me to go to his mosque...

you know...to a youth event. And before you say no, DeeDee agreed to go with me."

My mom, the woman who always has something to say, doesn't make a sound.

So, I wait.

And wait.

And wait some more.

Right before my insides explode, she answers. "It's up to you. If you're sure, then go."

Wait a minute. She's really okay with this?

"...Thank you." There's so much I want to add, but her arms are crossed tight over her chest. "I'll get you the details soon."

Maybe she can help pick an appropriate outfit. Aside from jeans and cargo pants, I only own miniskirts, and seeing how much skin Aunt Samira covers up...well, a quick shopping trip to my favorite consignment store might be necessary. Because I have to get this right. I have to.

If the people in my grandfather's community accept me, maybe he will too.

Maybe even my aunt will.

"I'm going to take a shower." Mom rises and takes a few steps before turning back to me. "Your report card was posted online. A solid B average is fine to me, but don't mention it to your grandfather. He's much more critical—I should know."

CHAPTER
EIGHT

December

DeeDee hands me the box. "Did you order something online?"

"No," I tell her. "Maybe it was sent here by mistake."

"But the package is addressed to you."

I grab a pair of scissors and saw through the packing tape. From inside, my fingers fish out a card. Its handwritten note explains all:

Salaam, Leena,
After you helped me with my computer, I thought it would be a good thing if you had an upgrade to your own.
Enjoy,
Your grandfather Tariq.

I clear the packing peanuts to reveal a glossy box. "He sent me a new *laptop*?"

"Duh. Let's talk about what we *don't* already know," DeeDee says, pushing back against the obvious. "Like, how are you telling your mom about this?"

Carrying a handful of her favorite licorice, Mom appears over us. "I'm listening."

Damn. Didn't even get a little time to decide whether to lie or not.

"Well...first you've gotta know...I didn't ask for this in any way." My words stumble out. "During my visit to Tariq's house this past Sunday, I helped him with some basic computer stuff...and now..."

I hold up the laptop package.

"Of course he did this. Three days is impressive. It's all part of his plan to get in good with you. Once you're hooked, his *small advice* or *tiny nudges* won't seem so bad. They will be, and they'll get worse, but you'll convince yourself that he's being helpful." Her cheeks turn bright red. "We'll all be able to enjoy Samira's digs about the neighborhood we live in, or the inappropriate clothes I buy you too!"

"I think I should go," DeeDee says, shooting off the sofa. "I'll be back tomorrow."

After she slips out, my mom and I stare at each other. "So, do you want me to give it back?"

Mom's gaze shifts away, while she continues drumming her fingers on the burgundy fabric of the couch. The longer I wait for her to answer, the harder my heartbeat thumps in my chest.

Breathe, girl, breathe.

Facing forward, she says, "As much as I *want* to say, 'Return it,' that's not my decision. Keep it or not. Just remember: NOTHING comes from my family without steel strings attached."

Why? Why can't this be a good thing? "Aren't you even a little bit happy for me?"

Instead of answering, she heads into the kitchen.

Really?

I hurry after her. "Ma, can't we talk about this? Really talk? You've always said no topic is off-limits!"

Still silence.

After setting the oven to four hundred degrees, she lines up some fish sticks in two perfect rows, then slices handfuls of cherry tomatoes on a plastic cutting board. "Leena, do you really want to know?"

Only a second passes. "Yes. I do."

She pushes out a sigh.

"I'll start from the beginning. My mother died when I was fifteen. But before that, my childhood was amazing. I was a sporty kid. After watching tae kwon do in the summer Olympics, I was hooked—I wanted *so* much to try it. So, at eleven, Mom found me a woman-owned dojang. Best four years of my life."

"Were you any good?" Trying to imagine my mother kicking someone in the head or breaking a board is crazy.

"And I was getting better every practice. Your grandmother, Nadia, took me to all the local martial arts competitions, and I usually placed in them. Sometimes, even Dad was proud of me."

Tingles run up and down my arms and legs. Nadia. Her name was Nadia.

"When Mom passed...things changed. Two weeks after the funeral, Aunt Samira moved in with us. My dad kept himself busy, but when he wasn't working, he started going to the local masjid more. At first, just on Fridays for the weekly congregational prayer. That turned into making the last of the five daily prayers there every evening. He left his sister in charge of the house—*and* of me."

Swallowing my fear, I ask something I need to know. "Was it really that bad? With Aunt Samira, I mean?"

Her glassy eyes tell me everything.

"My mother and Samira weren't friends. They had different ideas about religion. Nadia always told me that treating others respectfully is the single best way for Muslims to show how great Islam is. Covering her hair or wearing all black weren't things she did."

"Wait, did you *ever* wear something on your head?"

"Nope. My mom believed that hijab was a personal decision each Muslim woman had to make for herself." She points at my hair. "Don't think Samira won't be after you. It was one of the first things she tried to push on me, and when I refused...it didn't go over well. There's more, too, but that's for later."

That explains a lot. Not everything, but a lot.

Still, I'm not intimidated. I can handle Aunt Samira. I know I can. After all, she's never done anything to me—not really. She must have changed.

"Ma, all of that sounds bad, but don't you want to give them another chance?" I inch closer to her. "It's been more than a decade. They're family. And I think they're—"

"Look, Leena, they might have changed, but I doubt it. My aunt is stuck in her ways. I can accept that—but my *own father* allowed his sister to destroy our relationship." She gives me a long, hard look. "One day, he might apologize. I'm fine without him until then."

CHAPTER
NINE

December

As Deidre and I pick up every toy from the living room floor, my mom wipes down both high chairs parked at the kitchen table. She clears her throat several times in a row. DeeDee and I glance at each other, knowing something is coming.

"Leena, make sure to ask Samira if she expects both of you to cover your hair. I'd hate for it to be a surprise."

DeeDee is the first to open her mouth. "Is she *serious*?"

I have no clue. "Don't freak out. I'll ask."

"Good, 'cause I'm not down to dress like a nun to go to this thing!"

Going alone *can't happen*, so after putting on my fakest, most confident grin, I say, "Whatever we wear will be fine, I'm sure. But I'll text Samira and verify."

My mom walks over. "We'll all wait together to hear."

My fingers quiver as I type:

> Hi, Samira. Is there a dress code for the youth event tomorrow?

My palms are damp.

It only takes a minute for her to reply.

> Salaam, Leena. The Imam's wife assured me that the non-Muslim teens attending can wear what they want. But please, as a favor to your grandfather, can you at least NOT wear super tight clothes?

I shoot back an answer.

> Thanks. Don't worry, I'll tell my best friend & we can both wear baggy jeans. See you there!

> Oh, you're not coming alone? I'll let them know to expect two of you. Please be there by 5 p.m. Salaam.

"So??" My mom's a little too eager.

Ignoring her smug excitement, I announce, "Jeans are fine. We're good, DeeDee."

I take it as a good sign.

Mom shrugs.

Here's hoping that everything else goes smoothly.

≈

By four p.m. on Saturday, I'm still standing in front of my closet in a bathrobe.

"Ugh." After one last look, I walk to my door and crack it open. "MA, I have absolutely nothing to wear. HELP!"

A whole minute later, she joins me. "Why are you stressing about this?" She points to the blue argyle sweater. "What about that? It's loose enough not to make your aunt frown."

She's a magician.

I dress in a hurry after that. Once I have on the oversized sweater and the only pair of non-ripped blue jeans in my closet, I move on to doing something with my hair. I run my brush through it several times and pull my thick mane into a ponytail, then secure it with a huge blue scrunchie.

After yanking on a pair of socks, I grab my low-top Converse and my phone, then pause in front of the bathroom mirror. I look pretty good—at least, I think so. With minty breath and shiny lip gloss applied, I head into the living room. As I tie my sneaks, there's a hard knock at the door.

Before I can stand, my mom rushes past me and lets Deidre in. She's wearing a black sweater, white jeans, and a puffer jacket—finds from our favorite secondhand store. Her light brown complexion is stunning as usual. I wish my face was as free of acne as hers.

"Damn, girls. You both look cute!" Since whistling isn't one of her talents, my mom snaps her fingers in the air. "But where you're going, that won't matter."

I gift her my best give-it-a-rest glare. Not sure if it's ever worked. "You ready, DeeDee?"

My BFF shakes her head. "No, but let's do this."

"Not that I'm super concerned about the crowd you'll be around, but, Leena, if you can't be home by eleven p.m., please text me."

"I will, Ma. Bye."

We head outside and into DeeDee's car. As soon as we pull out of our driveway, DeeDee asks her single burning question. "Is there going to be food at this thing?"

My girl is always hungry.

"Samira mentioned snacks, but anything more than that, I'm not sure." Holding up my phone, I ask, "Do you want me to ask?"

"Nah." She takes the next exit—and four right turns later, I have the answer. As we pull into the mosque's huge parking lot, we see the back half blocked off. I count three barbecue grills and five food trucks.

"Damn, do you smell that?" Deidre asks, parking.

I check myself one last time in the rearview mirror before getting out. "At least the food will be great."

"Leena! *Leena!*"

We both turn in the direction of my name. Aunt Samira is approaching us, wearing the same black ankle-length dress I saw at the hospital. (Of course, she makes an obvious visual inspection of our clothing. She has no shame.)

"Hi, Samira! This is my best friend, Deidre." I look around. "Where's Tariq?"

DeeDee mumbles, "Hello."

My aunt says, "Nice to meet you." Turning more towards me, she answers, "He overdid things this week. So your grandfather stayed home to rest. But I'll be here with both of you." She takes a few steps towards the mosque. "Follow me, girls."

We do as we're told and enter into a large space with three tall shoe racks lining the closest wall. "You can put your shoes here."

My BFF nudges me, but all I can do is shrug and follow Samira's instructions.

It could be me being paranoid...but every Muslim teenage girl in the room turns to look at us. None of them is dressed like us. They're all wearing some variation of an ankle-length dress and a colorful head covering.

But I notice one beaming brown face among them. She, at least, smiles at us.

A few guys are there, too, but they're playing a game on the ping-pong table in a corner of the room. Seeing the rows of soda and sparkling water, they must be expecting more than a hundred students.

Samira stops at an empty table. "Here we go. You can sit here, and I'll go find the organizer. She really wants to meet you, Leena."

With that, we are on our own.

76

We sit in the hard plastic chairs. I scoot mine close to Deidre. "What do you think?"

"L, someone's trying to get your attention," she says, pointing towards the door.

Ray from my tenth-grade AP English is standing by the shoe rack. And he's waving—yuck. But his cute friend is there too. But Mo never looks in our direction. Instead, they both head through another set of double doors.

"Who's that?" Deidre whispers in my ear. "An admirer you've been keeping a secret?"

The thought turns my empty stomach. "Gross. I told you about Raymond. He's a major pain in the ass. And his cute friend doesn't go to our school." I keep my gaze on the doors they went through.

"So . . . you interested?"

"In Ray? No thanks."

She taps the table in front of me. "No, silly. In his *friend*. You can't stop smiling."

Touching the upturned sides of my mouth, I can't lie. "He's kinda fit, but I don't know anything about him."

"Yet."

Before I can tell her how wrong she is, Aunt Samira is back. And she's not alone. "Leena and Deidre, this is Sister Maryam. She's the Imam's wife and the organizer of this youth event."

The lady with my aunt is super tall, but her smile is even bigger. Her pink skirt and knee-length tunic are just as bright as her white headscarf. "Hello! I'm so pleased both of you are here today. After a short talk, the fun will start. Have either of you ever been to a mosque?"

DeeDee just shakes her head, but I say, "No, ma'am. Are we dressed okay?"

The grimace on Samira's face gives me a second of regret.

But Sister Maryam's warm green gaze relaxes the tightness in my shoulders. "Please don't worry. You two are fine—but thank you so much for asking." She turns. "Samira, we might need a second person at the soft cookie station. Is that something you can help with?"

"Of course. As long as I can keep an eye on my niece." Oh, great. She's serious about her chaperoning duties. Not knowing what to say, I pick at my cuticles under the table.

"Ma'am, is the stuff from the food trucks really expensive?" This question is typical DeeDee.

The Imam's wife chuckles. "Due to our generous community, all the games and the food are free."

Deidre's grin can't get any bigger. "Wow, thanks."

"I hope these young people appreciate all of this," Aunt Samira adds. "It cost a lot."

Way to ruin the vibe.

A super tall man props open the double doors. "As-salaamu alaykum and welcome! Imam Yahya is almost ready to begin."

Sister Maryam raises her voice. "InshaALLAH, if everyone will follow me into our large prayer space. The young men will sit to the left while the young ladies will join me to the right."

The room we follow her into is carpeted in navy blue, imprinted with elaborate designs. I've never seen anything like it. There's not a single piece of furniture, so everyone sits on the floor, and DeeDee and I follow suit. Sister Maryam and my aunt settle in right behind us. A few of the Muslim girls sneak glances at us but turn around when an older man appears at the front.

"As-salaamu alaykum, and welcome to everyone joining us." His smile is calming. "My name is Imam Yahya Suleiman. I am delighted to see so many of the community's young people here tonight. We've invited some local young people, too, to demonstrate what our place of worship looks like—and even let you have a little fun." He scans the large space, then asks, "To our visitors tonight: Has anyone ever been to a masjid before?"

From his spot across the room, Ray raises his hand. He's the only one.

"It's okay if you haven't." The Imam takes a few steps forward. "This is where we hold our congregational prayers. Muslims are required to pray five times a day, and our mosque is open every day for whoever wants to perform those here."

Some guy comes out of a side door, carrying a folding chair. You can't miss the word SECURITY printed in bold black letters on his neon vest. He sets the seat down beside the Imam.

"Today, my very short talk concerns the importance of education in Islam." Imam Yahya sits. "Education is so important in our faith that it's obligatory for *every* Muslim to seek knowledge. It's not something that a person is more or less entitled to based on their family, social status, or gender. Everyone is—"

Before he can continue, one of the guys sporting a high-top mid-fade raises his hand. Everyone turns.

"Yes?" the imam asks, no sign of irritation.

"What about men in Muslim countries who want to stop girls going to school?" His question makes sense. Even I've read online articles about places like Afghanistan.

Behind us, Aunt Samira mumbles under her breath.

But Imam Yahya still has a smile on his face. "Without bringing politics into this talk, please remember that some people are more guided by culture—and, unfortunately, that affects how they practice their faith. I, for one, pray that with more *education*, things like that will cease to exist for Muslims."

I think what he's saying might be true. I've only known my grandfather for, like, a month, and he's already pushing me to focus more on college. He doesn't fit the stereotype.

"As I was saying: Education is *so* important in our faith that it's the duty of anyone with knowledge to teach what they know to others. And that's not limited to men—it's incumbent on all Muslims. I want to share this truth with you all. I hope you will consider it as you begin thinking about college and your majors."

Sounds great, but we're sitting on our side of the room, and the guys are on the other.

I don't get it.

Instead of asking why myself, I lean over and whisper into my best friend's ear: "Ask why we're not allowed to sit beside the guys."

Her hand shoots straight up. "Can you explain why we're separated like this?" Deidre points to where the boys are seated.

The whispers between a pair of Muslim girls in front of us are *way* too obvious. Their sneers zero in on DeeDee. I gulp. It's my question, but she's catching heat for it.

The Imam's calm expression hasn't changed. "That's a great question. In Islam, there's no dating like what's done here in the US. A young man and young lady will only have in-depth conversations for the purpose of determining if they are suitable for marriage, and both families are involved, as a protection for everyone.

"That said, even though we arranged our seating like this, tonight's event will be one where all of you can interact with each other. With the correct supervision, of course."

I could ask many more questions, but after a quick glance over my shoulder, Aunt Samira's frosty glare convinces me to keep my mouth shut. I'm sure she saw me prod DeeDee to ask that question.

Looking around the room, Imam Yahya stands. "The carnival outside is now open. There's dinner food, snacks, and popcorn to enjoy. Have fun! And if you have any questions about the faith, please, come and speak to me."

DeeDee doesn't need a second invitation to eat. She's on her feet a few seconds later. "Come on, let's check out the food trucks!"

We're back in our shoes and outside in record time. After crossing the parking lot, I park myself at one of the picnic tables closest to a tall portable heater, while Deidre rushes to the nearest food truck. Before I figure out what I'm eating, she's back, the smell of garlic and spices making my stomach growl.

"Girl, samosas and daal? I'm in heaven."

My mouth drops open. "I didn't know you liked Indian food!"

"My grandmother hates how it smells and doesn't allow it in the house, so I don't eat it a lot." Deidre points at her already half-empty plate. "You should get some, it's amazing!"

More people are joining us outside, so I rush over to the line.

Ray and his friend Mo walk past me. The slight Albuquerque wind does nothing to dispel the sudden wave of warmth spreading across my face at the sight of them. But I wonder if Mo would even talk to me after what the Imam said.

DeeDee grabs one of my fries and eats it. "Damn, those are great."

"Hey, Leena."

Ugh. Ray's voice is the *last* thing I want to hear. On the bright side, Ray's hot friend is *also* standing by our table.

"Hi," I say.

"It's great food, am I right?" Ray parks himself at the picnic table right next to us. At least he's closer to DeeDee (sorry, DeeDee). "Oh, this is Mo. You remember him?"

His crown of curly black hair captures all my attention, so my bestie saves me. "Hey, Mo, I'm Deidre, Leena's friend." She kicks me under the table, hard.

"It's nice to see you again." Sounding as stiff as if I'm interviewing for a part-time job at Sonic isn't doing me any favors.

Ray gazes at DeeDee. "Wow—you are pretty. How have we not met properly?"

Raymond will find out the hard way my best friend is not interested in dating anyone at our high school.

"We haven't met because I don't care to make the acquaintance of every smelly boy at the institution," DeeDee says sweetly. "So, Mo, tell us something about you. How many siblings do you have?"

"I'm the youngest of five." I bet Muhammad's four siblings are great—always someone to talk to and have fun with. Not that I'd really know.

"How about you two?"

My BFF points from me to her. "We're both only children but closer than most sisters."

He smiles, beautifully, then turns to his friend. "Ray, I'm heading in to pray maghrib. You staying here?"

Shaking his head, Ray stands. "I'll come—no one's really that interesting here."

I watch as Deidre's fingers wrap around her fork in a death grip. "Right back at you."

Mo hands Ray his plate. "Here, hold this. Make sure you finish your food while you're waiting for me; your hunger is affecting your judgment." He turns to me. "If the two of you check out the carnival, maybe we'll see you again in a few minutes."

"Yes. Great. Yes." My words tumble out.

Watching him walk back towards the mosque, I catch Aunt Samira's hard stare. Her pursed lips hint that another conversation with a Muslim boy isn't something she wants to happen.

My newfound family is nothing like the mom who's raising me.

Not sure if that's a good thing or not.

CHAPTER
TEN

December

The cool night air must have softened her heart (or the long winding line of teenagers waiting for chocolate chip cookies from her stand is a distraction) because Aunt Samira doesn't beetle over and order us to leave after pseudo-flirting.

"Let's check out the games!" DeeDee announces.

I don't let my cold hands stop me from following her to the second parking lot on the other side of the building. As someone with no interest or ability in sports, I glide right past the basketball hoop challenge.

Deidre's chuckles ring in my ears.

"Ha, ha. Not all of us can make a three-pointer." We're right beside something called the Balloon Pop Challenge. "Let's try this one instead."

The white-haired older man in front of the wall of inflated balloons arranged in three rows smiles in my direction. "Hello there. Can I interest you in one of our prizes?"

Above his head are furry teddy bears, stuffed pandas with large heads, and plush pastel stars.

With no track record of winning anything, I take the plunge. "Sure."

DeeDee cracks her gum. "This I HAVE to see."

The noisy carnival chatter surrounding us disappears. I glance around, expecting a spotlight to shine on the booth.

"Here you go, young lady." The older guy running the game hands me four darts. "Now, all you have to do is pop three balloons out of four tries to win the prize of your choice."

I tune out his safety instructions and the short tutorial on the best way to throw a dart.

"Any questions?"

"Nope."

Squaring up my shoulders, my feet dig into the pavement. "Here goes nothing," I tell DeeDee. With one eye open, I release the first dart.

"You got this," my BFF claps back as my throw hits its target.

One balloon down.

After stepping close to the portable heater and warming up my hands, I return to my original position. I check to my left and to my right—no Aunt Samira in sight. A breeze blows across my thick ponytail. I send the second red dart flying and some magical force must have helped it because it's another miracle.

Two balloons down.

The stuffed star might end up coming home with me.

"Isn't this interesting?" Ray's sarcasm breaks my fledgling confidence. Out of the corner of my eyes, I catch him and Muhammad standing close to Deidre.

For a minute, giving up is a real possibility. I'm not a show pony. I don't want to perform in front of him.

But when I glance from Ray's smug smirk to Mo's kind eyes, my insides turn over twice.

"You can't be serious!" My bestie shoots at Ray. "Shut up. She's already made two perfect shots."

"Nah. Leena isn't the sporty type—anyone can make a lucky shot."

Extra saliva fills my mouth. I force it down and wind up my arm. Next the dart sails out of my hand.

And into the space between two balloons.

"See! I called it!" Ray crows.

Guys like him are the worst.

"Ray, back off. It's supposed to be fun." Mo walks over to me, holding his hand out. "Dart, please."

I hand it to him, while trying to hear anything over the deafening pounding of my heart.

"Can I take her last shot?" he asks the older man.

"As long as the young lady doesn't mind."

Mo gifts me a teeth-baring smile. "Do you?"

The woodsy scent of his body spray steals my words, so I just shake my head.

He takes a single step forward, plants his feet shoulder-width apart, and, without aiming, sails the last dart straight into the middle of one of the balloons.

Pop!

"Great job, young man." The older guy turns to me. "Which prize would you like?"

He's pointing to all of them but I already know which one is my favorite.

But, really, I already have my prize. Mo's right beside me, smiling at me. His body heat warms my insides—it might be a permanent temperature change. "I'd like one of the stuffed stars. The light blue one."

"Girlie, another star? You're too much. Aren't the star-shaped sticky notes, erasers, and notebooks enough?"

"*Hush.*" I give her my best death stare. "Big mouth."

The cheesy grin on Muhammad's face tells me he heard. "Interesting what some people collect. One of my older sisters is addicted to panda toys."

Maybe... just maybe... he doesn't think I'm too weird, then.

"Where's Ray?" he asks. "Did he leave?"

She nods towards the building. "I didn't look at the time when he walked away."

Mo laughs a little. "What's next for the two of you?"

Before I can answer, DeeDee does. "I'm itching to try out the basketball shoot-out. Care to put a small bet on who scores the most points?"

This time, it's on me to step in. "Don't do it! Deidre has been playing since sixth grade. Last year, she was the only freshman on our school's varsity team."

He raises his hands in surrender. "In that case, I think I'm good. I know a winner when I see one."

I wink. He winks back.

With DeeDee leading the way, she and I head to the shooting booth. Someone is already shooting, but each time the ball misses the hoop. She's wearing sweat pants, an oversized long full-zip hoodie, and a headscarf.

"Is this game rigged? Some of these shots should be going in."

"No, it's not. I've given out a dozen prizes tonight." The tall woman manning the booth keeps a blank face. "Want to try again?"

"I'm done."

The complainer steps to the side and DeeDee walks up. "The rules?"

"To win a prize, you have to get four out of five shots into the basket." The woman holds up a ball. "Interested?"

"Oh, yeah."

Once my bestie has the basketball, the smile drops off her face. She's laser-focused on the target. After adjusting her position, Deidre shoots. The ball *sails* into the hoop.

Not just once.

Every single time.

"MashaALLAH, you weren't lying! She's good!" Muhammad reappears right at my side, his eyes wide. "Hey, are you still on the team, DeeDee?"

The last girl to shoot—the no-talent one—is way too interested in our conversation. She sidles closer to hear what he's saying to me and DeeDee.

"I love playing," DeeDee explains, "but all the time for practice and the games dropped my grades so Lilian made me stop."

"She lives with her grandmother," I explain to Muhammad.

Our uninvited guest jumps in. "You were on a team? That's not fair." Pointing at my bestie, she says acidly, "You're like a *professional*. There should be different rules for people like you."

The chilly breeze strengthens. My shoulders tense.

"People like *me*?" DeeDee glares at this girl. "What the fuck does that mean?"

Muhammad jumps in between the pair. "Everyone needs to chill."

But the girl refuses to back down—she plants her hands on her hips. "I heard you—being on a varsity team should disqualify you from getting a prize."

Deidre's calm nature is deceptive—she goes from zero to one sixty in a blink. Her nostrils flare. "Are you really hung up on some cheap-ass carnival prizes? Like you need a stupid set of inflated bobbleheads. Give me a break!"

Putting my hand over hers, I whisper, "Forget her. Let's get some chocolate chip cookies."

I have to drag her to the opposite end of the row of carnival games.

It takes a few minutes before she shakes off her angry, kill-you face. "Somebody didn't get the message about how you treat guests. Do you think your aunt will give me two cookies? I need a serious sugar fix."

I pivot towards Muhammad. "You coming too?"

He nods. "Gotta find Ray, then we'll see you over there."

I move my feet faster to keep up with DeeDee's longer stride. "You can't help that your superior shooting skills make others jealous."

The closer we get to the chocolate chip cookie stand, the clearer I can see Aunt Samira's face. Her lips are flat, and she keeps glaring in our direction.

"Hi, Samira. Can DeeDee and I each have two warm cookies, please?"

Her cool gaze appraises us. "Unfortunately, the rule is only one per person. That way, there's enough for everyone." After handing each of us our chocolate chip cookies, she adds, "So, were you trying to make our family look bad on purpose, or is arguing in public something you enjoy doing?"

Her hostility is a nasty shock.

"Miss Stewart, please don't blame Leena. She didn't do anything wrong." DeeDee sounds sincere, polite. "That girl started it. But we both walked away."

I add, "That's the truth."

Aunt Samira's RBF doesn't budge. "InshaALLAH, we'll discuss it later."

Taking her words as a dismissal, we work our way over to an empty picnic table farthest away from everyone. The super sweet chocolate turns bitter in my mouth. "I'm so sorry, DeeDee."

"Don't worry. It's not your fault . . . but I'm out." She hasn't touched her chocolate chip cookie. "You coming?"

Glancing back, I sigh. "Naw. That'd be great, but my aunt wants to talk later."

DeeDee pops a stick of gum in her mouth. "And you're okay with that? She was *really* hard on you."

I shrug. "Guess I have to be. Isn't this normal family stuff?"

"Nothing about this is normal. I mean, damn, you just found out two members of your mom's family live in Santa Fe and are Muslim—that's deep."

Grabbing my half-eaten carnival treat, I get up. The thousand things swirling in my brain distract me, and I toss it into the closest trash can.

"Hey, I could've taken that home."

"Sorry." As soon as I sit down again, I say, "My mom ran away from all of this."

My bestie snaps her fingers inches from my face. "Not very far. Girl, look at where we are."

I scan the area filled with a small sea of teenage girls in headscarves and guys in small groups, with no interaction between the two. But most of them are smiling and laughing anyway.

"Just don't be too surprised if Samira pushes you in that direction." Deidre frees herself from the picnic table. "Text me when you get home. I'll stay up to hear how everything went."

Watching her car leave the parking lot, my throat dries up. I head back into the building and snag a bottle of water. I'm almost back to my seat when I notice Muhammad heading my way. Unfortunately, my aunt gets here first.

"Salaam, Leena. Did your friend leave?"

Peering over her shoulder, I watch Muhammad turn, heading in the opposite direction. "Yeah, she had to go. You can give me a ride home, right?"

"InshaALLAH, yes. Just let me tell the Imam's wife we're leaving."

My plan to find Muhammad and actually say goodbye is dashed when Aunt Samira and Sister Maryam are chatting it up at the edge of the picnic tables.

The imam's wife catches my eyes and waves.

I give her a weak one back.

Not two minutes later, Samira is back. "Are you ready?"

"Yes, ma'am."

She leads me to her her SUV. We're only just barely out of the parking lot before it begins.

"I know now it wasn't your friend who started the argument. But engaging in that kind of behavior *at all* doesn't look good for your grandfather or the Stewart family."

This woman is a little bent.

I squeeze my stuffed star, daring to talk back. "But...you blamed DeeDee immediately, when it was the Muslim girl's fault. What's her problem, anyway?"

Samira's gaze is locked on the road in front of us. "I don't know the family, but Sister Maryam is going to talk to her mother." Her sharp tone cuts. Damn, it wasn't that big of a deal.

"You spent entirely too much time with the young Muhammad Ameen. Was it really that difficult to heed the Imam?"

"No, no, Aunt Samira—it was all very innocent! He was just being nice to me and DeeDee."

Part of me wishes now that Mom had come with me. She would've dealt with this.

"Please consider how you act in public in the future."

I clear my throat, hoping to change the topic. "How is Tariq?"

Her grip on the steering wheel loosens up a little. "Alhamdulillah, he's getting a little stronger every day. Except, when he overdoes it, like today. Your grandfather is a great man."

At least he's not overly judgmental like some people.

"And you should know this. That young man is from a good family—not someone who would disobey his parents and have a girlfriend."

The more I defend myself, the longer she'll keep talking, so I bite my tongue, hard. Checking the cross streets, we only have a couple of minutes left together.

She pulls into the driveway, and I push the door open within seconds. "Thank you for the ride."

I escape her sedan, but before the door is closed, Samira pushes the button to lower the passenger window. "InshaAL-LAH, I hope you learned some new things tonight."

Forcing the sides of my mouth up, I say, "More than expected."

≈

Hey, you home yet?

Been here about an hour.

The second after sending, I regret telling the truth.

I'll let you get back to your alone time.

Wait, DeeDee. Don't go. Needed a minute before texting 😭

95

Why? Was the ride home bad?

Samira hates me.

Did she SAY that?

Her words: Our behavior made the
Stewart family look bad.

Let it out. I know you want to.

According to Samira...I spent too much
time with Muhammad

Shit!!! She's too much!

We agree on that.

Wait, did you two get caught kissing?

My cheeks warm at the silly question.

Of course not. I don't know him like that.

Then what happened?

Less than should have.

Nothing. But Samira didn't hear anything coming out of my mouth.

Guessing you didn't tell Asiyah?

Uh NO, I'm not that stupid

You should—your mom could help

Or forbid me from seeing my aunt and my grandfather.

If Samira is treating you foul, maybe it's the best thing.

Now my stomach's churning.

Dee, I gotta go. My mom needs something.

Liar. Love u. Later 😜

I drop my phone on the pillow beside me, a wave of guilt rolling over me.

Lying to my BFF isn't my go-to, *ever*, but giving up something I've wanted my entire life isn't part of the plan.

CHAPTER
ELEVEN

January

"Did my mom already give you the list of things we're supposed to get?"

"What's the face for?" Deidre asks, frowning at me. Powerful Albuquerque sunlight pours into the kitchen. "This sour attitude is about Samira. Tell me I'm wrong."

I'm too tired to lie. The way Samira treated me really fucking hurt. I don't even feel like myself this morning.

I mean, it is a new year.

It must be too much to ask to sleep until nine on Saturdays.

"Maybe. I mean, what can I do about her, anyway? Talking to my grandfather will make things impossible." I get up, shove my paper breakfast plate in the trash, and lean against the closest wall. "Ugh."

"Your mom needs to know. It's her family too."

A burning anger rises inside me. "Why do you *always* take her side? You're so obsessed with my mom, I swear. Are you my best friend or hers?"

The flash of surprise on her face doesn't last long. "Being your best friend means I get to tell you the truth, even if it's hard and might piss you off." She stands her ground, her arms crossed.

"Is it truth we're diving into? How about this? *You're jealous of me*—that's why you're always agreeing with my mom. No matter how many times you do it, it won't make you her daughter. That's a role already taken—by me."

Without another word, DeeDee grabs her phone and keys, her chair almost falling backwards. "Tell YOUR mom something came up and I can't work today."

Her icy glare slaps me. I should block the door and apologize until she forgives me, but shame freezes my feet in their spot.

I deserve her anger.

I'm curled up on the couch when the creak of my mom's door tells me round two is about to start. "Where's Deidre? I have the shopping list right here for you." She's holding a single sheet of notebook paper. "I don't hear the water in the kitchen running either."

I swallow down my nerves. "She left."

Her eyes widen. "Is she coming back?"

"Doubt it."

"What happened? Deidre is reliable." My mom's jaw hardens—she knows it's all my fault.

The springs in our *vintage* couch poke me in the spine. Even they know I'm in deep. "We had an argument and she walked out."

She collapses on the opposite end of the sofa. "Perfect. Two couples are stopping by in thirty minutes to see if Asiyah's Angels is a good fit for their first graders." Her eyes pierce me. "I don't have time for this today."

"I didn't tell her to leave! That was her decision."

"Whatever. If this disagreement is personal, then it's between the two of you. But it's affecting this business, so fixing it is your responsibility. NOW!"

She expects me to work a miracle.

The second after she goes into the kitchen, I race into my bedroom.

Unexpectedly, my phone rings—it's my grandfather. After staring at the screen for a second, I answer.

"Hi, Tariq. How are you feeling today?"

"Salaam, Leena. I'm much better, thank you for asking. Are you busy?"

Looking around my empty room, I say, "I don't think so."

"We need to talk about yesterday, specifically the things my sister said to you."

Here it is. He knows I behaved "badly." Now, he's going to tell me more horrible things. Maybe even leave my life as fast as he entered it.

"First, I must apologize for her words—they weren't nice. You and your friend didn't deserve them."

I swear the sunshine streaming into my room becomes brighter. "Did you...hear what she said from her last night?"

"I heard from two brothers who were there last night."

Wait, what? "Wow. So I've become a topic of conversation."

"No, nothing like that. It's rare that members of our community have non-Muslim grandchildren and they come to the masjid"—there's a break in his reply. "Are you interested in Muhammad Ameen?"

Why is *everyone* asking me that?

"We had a couple conversations. I'm sorry, but that doesn't mean I want to marry him." This is unreal. "He's just nice." Should I be offended or flattered right now? "Did I break some rule?"

"No, his father and I already spoke this morning. Mr. Ameen and I have been friends for many years."

This is beyond crazy. "Is he in trouble with his parents, because of me?"

"Of course not. Both families are just making sure nothing inappropriate happens in the future."

"Like...it's for my protection?"

"Exactly."

Not sure if I should say thanks.

"So, Leena, will you have time to visit me this week?"

"What about Samira? She doesn't like me..."

"Family is important to both me and my sister. Sometimes, she doesn't demonstrate it in the best way."

Damn right. And yet...why am I important and welcomed, but not my mom? I'm not brave enough to ask.

"InshaALLAH, text me later this week and let me know what time on either Thursday or Friday is better for you."

"Okay."

Voices from the front of the house drift into my room.

I recognize my mother's fake laugh. Not wanting to meet whoever she's interviewing, I'm trapped within these four walls. With DeeDee pissed at me, my only solution is to pick up a book and lose myself in its fantasy world.

Too bad all my problems can't be solved this way.

"Salaam, Leena."

I'm only four chapters in when my mom knocks, then enters my room. She's standing right inside the door, glaring at me.

I swallow down my fear. "Yes?"

"Did you fix things with Deidre?"

After putting in my bookmark, I set the novel beside me on the bed. "She's going to need a minute. I...was very mean." My gut tells me I screwed up big time.

"Are you planning to share with me what happened, or should I guess?"

My eyes fall on the massive bookcase beside the window. Pointing to the desk chair, I say, "It's better if you sit down."

She does, so I continue.

"DeeDee got in a shouting match with one of the Muslim girls last Saturday night. It wasn't her fault, but Samira absolutely freaked out. So DeeDee left early, and I got a ride home from Samira, who told me *such behavior* looks bad on the Stewart family."

"Sounds very familiar."

My throat's desert-dry but I can't stop now. "There's more. I talked to one of the Muslim boys and Aunt Samira noticed. According to her, it was too much."

"Does this young man have a name?"

"Muhammad Ameen."

Her sly smile isn't a good sign. "So, is this Mo? The one you asked about before Thanksgiving."

Of course, she remembers. "...Yes."

"First, I'm glad to know you're at least being a little more social. The Muslims here in Albuquerque are more on the conservative side, and your aunt is part of that crowd. I'm sorry you had to deal with judgment, but I'm not surprised. Was your grandfather there?"

"No, he was tired. I'm not even Muslim, Mom...why would anyone care what I do?"

"Most Muslims wouldn't, but there are people in every faith community who believe a family's honor rests between a woman's legs." She gets up, then settles beside me on the bed. "In their narrow view, you have the added shame of being a child born to me, a teenage mother who wasn't married." She wraps her fingers around mine. "When Samira came to live with us and my dad retreated into religion, my *normal* life vanished."

She stares out the window. "You now see how unreasonable my aunt is. My mother was a beautiful person who I could talk to. Even about Islam. But by the time I was your age...Samira's way of doing things was too much for me."

I've got a tickle in my throat.

"Attending an Islamic school wasn't enough. I wore the hijab and did my five daily prayers...but when my dad took away martial arts, it killed me. My next test would've been for my black belt. But your grandfather, probably pushed by his sister, pulled me out of the sport that was my passion."

Even thinking that leaves a sour taste in my mouth. "*Why* would he do that?"

Her eyelids close for a few seconds. "Samira said more than once that young ladies shouldn't train with teenage boys and grown men. Your grandmother believed if I practiced enough, I could make the American Olympic team. But that dream died with her." A tear escapes her eye.

I wrap my arms around her. "Mommy, I'm so sorry."

She shifts backwards, breaking our physical connection. "It's in the past. Being pregnant at sixteen, having to work and study for my GED...After you were born, I had to worry about providing for you. My priorities shifted."

"Do you...regret having me?"

Her tears spill over. "Of course not! Waiting would've been better, so we didn't struggle so much—but I wouldn't go back and do anything different. I adore you."

"Have you ever...Would you consider...We could get to know them, *together*. It's been almost twenty years, Mom."

The sadness on her face changes, deepens. "Thank you for inviting me to do this with you, but HELL NO."

It's like an emotional helium balloon popped between us.

"Mommy, what if they've changed?"

Her hardened jaw isn't a good sign. "Good for them—my answer is still the same."

"I don't get it. Will you ever forgive them?" My voice is a whisper. "I don't get why you won't even try."

"Why are you pushing them on me? You want to get to know them, fine. I'm allowing it. That should be enough." Her harsh words fracture my heart.

"But our whole family could crumble. Disappear. What happens then?"

She's staring at me, but nothing's coming out of her mouth.

I can't wait any longer. "Mother?" My breath turns shallow while beads of sweat dot my forehead. "Do you want me to never see them again? Will that make you happy?"

"Leena, you're old enough to decide for yourself."

"I appreciate that."

"Then you need to let me make my own choices too. The three of us have been through a ton of stuff you know nothing about—I made sure of that."

"But don't I deserve to know?"

An ocean of crimson spreads from one side of her face to the other. "I've already told you quite a lot today. Now who's being selfish? Listen, I was sixteen and made a tough decision that changed both of our lives." She's shaking. "So be pissed at me; that's on you. But never think you're owed *anything* from a situation you know next to nothing about."

My body's numb. All I can do is sit here and go along for the ride.

She gets up, heads to the door, then pivots. Her anger-filled eyes make me shudder. "Just don't complain to me when the Stewarts want to change you, insisting their dreams for your life should replace your own. I've always hated saying I told you so."

CHAPTER
TWELVE

January

My aunt and I agree on one thing: I don't fit in here.

My hair is uncovered, and I'm wearing a cheap, comfortable outfit, a cable-knit sweater and khakis. (But it's not like my ass is showing in a pair of short shorts. And what does it matter? The clothes on my back don't define me....Although my estranged family's Muslim community might disagree.)

But I'm here, helping the great-aunt I never knew I had, bringing a tray of snacks to strangers. Her guests, in her beautiful home, in Santa Fe.

"You can carry this, Leena," Samira announces, not a hint of a *please* in her tone.

Each of my hands grasp a side of the large porcelain platter, full of fancy chocolates wrapped in gold paper and an assortment of small cookies dusted with a light layer of cinnamon sugar. I can't help but think that a handful of Jolly Ranchers would be great right now.

Blowing out a stream of nervous energy, I put my *nothing-bothers-me* face on. This expression was perfected first in the fifth grade, when all my classmates talked about the

Father-Daughter Dance and how much fun it was going to be, how badly they wanted the perfect dress. Right now, just like that night, I'm being judged for something I have no control over.

I don't get it. In my entire sixteen years of existence, I've never killed anyone, stolen someone else's identity, or ditched a single class.

But...because my mom ran away and got pregnant with me, by a non-Muslim guy, these people think they can judge me as a mistake. A sin that should be hidden.

The thought of cursing out Aunt Samira's watchful guests flashes in my brain, but that's not a possibility.

"Leena, are you coming?" Samira's sharp reminder of my job pulls me out of my thoughts.

With just socks on, I step carefully along the dark wood floors behind my aunt, who's carrying mugs of floral-scented hot tea.

We enter the den with the strong Santa Fe sun streaming in from the floor-to-ceiling windows.

One look at the grin on Tariq's face as he meets my eyes melts away half my doubts for a few precious seconds. "Come, Leena," my grandfather calls to me. "Set the tray on the coffee table and let me introduce you to our guests."

The older man, who's sporting a bushy, black beard, and the woman beside him, dressed in a long, black flowing dress, both smile in my direction. With them is a teenager who looks like their daughter. She's wearing the same kind of loose, flowing clothing like her mom but cream colored, and she has nothing but indifference in her stare.

I follow the instructions, then sit next to my grandfather on his large, black leather sectional.

His hand rests on my shoulder for only a few seconds.

"Leena, this is one of my oldest friends, Amir, and his wife, Rashida." He motions towards Miss Angry Face. "And the lovely young lady is their daughter Rheem."

I manage a small wave and a smaller "Hi."

After a quick scan of my person, the girl returns a quick "Hello."

The couple greets me enthusiastically, especially the woman. "MashaALLAH, she looks so much like your daughter, Brother Tariq!"

A flash of sorrow passes over my grandfather's face. "I do see the resemblance, Rashida, but my granddaughter is much calmer and more open-minded than Asiyah," he says for all to hear. "Leena attended the teen event at the masjid and promised me she'll read some information about Islam."

My fingers grip the side of my pants. That was uncalled for.

"MashaALLAH, that's wonderful." Amir nods. "Unfortunately, Rheem had a babysitting job and couldn't attend the event."

Rheem's wide-eyed expression tells me she didn't expect to have to talk. "That's true, Abu, but a lot of my friends were there, and I heard *all* about it." Now she looks in my direction. I'd bet my next paycheck one of those friends is the one who had words with DeeDee.

After a short coughing episode and a sip of hot herbal tea, my grandfather is back in the conversation. "InshaALLAH, Leena will learn how to love our way of life more than her mother ever did. Our youth are the future, and I can't wait to see what ALLAH has planned for my only grandchild."

Wait a minute. Nothing about this is okay. He's expecting me to fill in as the dutiful daughter? A stand-in for my mom...no thanks.

Not.

Interested.

But maybe I'm wrong to expect him to be happy with *me*. To not want me to assume a role to make up for someone else's past.

"Alhamdulillah, I have the money to help Leena get accepted in a top university." His plans for my future terrify me. What is all this? "Such a blessing."

I gulp down some tea. *Just breathe.*

Samira jumps in. "Please have some of the goodies. Those biscochitos are divine. It's a traditional recipe, without the lard."

While everyone else digs in, I nurse my tea. Tariq can't put all of this on me and think I'll agree to it all. I don't want to believe my mom is right about him.

Whenever I scan the room, Aunt Samira is still watching me. I focus on the rose bush in their backyard to calm myself. I count backwards.

Nothing works.

"Leena, did you hear your grandfather?" My great-aunt's verbal shove brings me back.

Catching the concern on his face, I say, "No, I didn't. What's up?"

"Brother Amir and his family are leaving."

Refocusing on the group, I catch Rheem's haughty stare. Well, whatever. We share the same attitude.

The two men stand and embrace. "Jazak ALLAH khair for the visit." Tariq pivots to look me in the face. "Please go with Samira and walk them out."

Rashida grins. "Leena, it's a wonderful thing to see you and your grandfather connecting after all these years."

I'm surprised when Rheem waves at me before being the first one into the hallway.

"As-salaamu alaykum," Tariq says, his cheesy grin on full display.

The couple replies in unison, "Wa alaykum as salaam."

The second the front door closes behind them, my aunt turns to me. "Please say goodbye to your grandfather, then I'll drive you home."

She vanishes to the kitchen. I watch Tariq finishing one of the cookies. "You won't tell, will you, Leena? These biscochitos are so good. Have one." He points to the half-empty platter.

I grab a napkin. "My mom will eat them. Samira told me we're leaving."

My grandfather's shoulders aren't as straight as before. He pats the cushion beside him. "Come talk to me for just a few minutes." Following his instructions, I sit.

"I'd hoped you and Rheem would have talked more to each other, but inshaALLAH, your aunt gave Sister Rashida your phone number so you two young ladies can get together. Her family lives in Albuquerque."

He doesn't get it. "We probably don't have that much in common."

Tariq points to a diploma hanging on the wall across from us. "Leena, I thought maybe you could talk to her about college. MashaALLAH, she's already in her senior year of high school and plans to become a pediatrician. Rheem's been home-schooled until now. She'll be at home, attending an online school this coming fall and taking dual credit classes at CNM. Her dedication to education is impressive, don't you think?"

Is this about me, or my last name? "I guess so, yes." To escape this conversation, I stand and take two steps towards the door. "I don't want to keep Aunt Samira waiting."

"InshaALLAH, we'll see each other soon."

Am I stupid not to have expected this?

I clutch my phone; knowing what I've got to do doesn't make my heartbeat stop racing.

≈

Hey, what's up? You home?

I'm about to lose at solitaire for the third time when DeeDee finally replies.

Nothing much. Lilian is with some old guy at her regular casino. Ice cream is keeping me company ☠

Been there a couple of times.

Chocolate Chip Cookie Dough for dinner again?

You know it.

I hesitate.

I'm so, so, so sorry. Really.

Now, my forehead's damp.

No excuses. I fucked up.

And?

Damn. She's not making this easy.

I know you're not jealous of me. It's just annoying how right you always are. About everything.

Look, babe, I know you're going through it. But your mother GIVES a damn. You're more than a burden in her life.

We both know what she's talking about.

You're right. ALWAYS. What's Lilian saying these days?

Well...I let it slip about your new family.... Sorry. She was like "Leena has two strikes against her already—being Black and a woman—is she adding Muslim for a third strike?" Don't be surprised if she says that to your face one day!

How my bestie lives with her is beyond me.

> DeeDee...do you forgive me? I am truly so sorry.
> I love you. You know that.

Before I can look away, she types,

> I guess I'll forgive you this time...since you'd be
> like a tourist lost in the Sandias without me 🏃

Can't argue with that.

> Also! Missing out on a few hours of pay wasn't
> good for my bank account...let's not do that
> again, L

> Agreed!!!!

> Tell your mom I'm sorry about bailing.

> I will. I'm not her favorite person rn

> You apologizing to her too?

> Yes. Talk later

> Love u too ✦

CHAPTER
THIRTEEN

January

By Monday morning, the invisible emotional distance between me and my mom irks the hell out of me. You'd think volunteering to clean the hallway bathroom before the daycare kids get here on my MLK school holiday would earn me some brownie points, but she didn't even say thank you.

Has she ever?

I gather up the sponges. Once everything is put away, I head into the living room. DeeDee is parked on our couch.

"Living dangerously, I see. Eating on the furniture."

"Shhh...Your mom's in a good mood." My bestie points towards the kitchen.

The urge to run and tell her everything that's happened to me in the other part of my life eats at me.

By lunchtime, I've changed a couple newborn diapers, wiped two runny noses, and half-finished three coloring pages. DeeDee hands out the kids' plates while my mom feeds one of the infants her bottle.

Wandering over to the couch, my mom examines me. "Leena, you've got something on your uniform shirt. Can you please take care of it before one of the parents sees you?"

She places the baby against her shoulder, patting his back.

I glance down. The blob of strawberry jam isn't even that big. My feet haven't moved.

"Now, please!"

Arguing in front of the daycare kids is another no-no. I trudge into my room and change my T-shirt. Because it's sitting on my desk, I check my phone. There's a new notification from a local 505 number, so I open it.

> Hey, Leena, it's Rheem. We met at your grandfather's house.

It came in an hour ago.

Don't know what she wants, but a spark of curiosity drives me. We didn't really connect when we met in Santa Fe. I thought.

> Hi. I remember!

That's all I can manage for now. Since my mom's work rules are part of my DNA, the phone stays while I head back.

≈

By 4:30 p.m., it's just the three of us again, no kids. "I never want to hear 'The Itsy Bitsy Spider' ever again in life."

"Really? At least it's a classic," my mother says, standing in between me and DeeDee. "Your favorite shows growing up irked my last nerve every day."

"So why did you let me watch them over and over again?"

"They made you happy."

I scramble to my feet and crush my arms around her waist. The familiar scent of coconut body butter soothes me.

She stumbles backwards. "You okay?"

Holding back tears, I say, "Glad you're not still pissed."

She squeezes my shoulders. "It's been just us for so long. One disagreement isn't a big deal." She waves DeeDee in for the hug, then breaks the embrace. "Leena, please remember that the two of us are your family too. And Deidre and I can't be replaced."

My body is light enough to float away. "I know."

DeeDee's stomach growls. "Sorry, I haven't eaten in a while."

My mom looks at her. "No worries. I'll take care of that."

I laugh, then head for the hallway. "I need to check my phone. Be right back." In my room, I see a new text from Tariq. Instead of replying to that Rheem girl, I open his up.

Salaam, Leena. How are you today? I'm going for a walk at Quigley Park today. Would you like to meet me there?

Isn't it too chilly for you to walk outside? What time?

His reply is immediate.

> It's fifty-five degrees, not too cold. InshaALLAH, in thirty minutes.

I chew on my thumb, the nail short from repeated use.

> Okay. Won't be able to stay long.

> That's fine. See you soon, Leena.

I change out of my daycare uniform shirt and into a turtleneck, a wool skirt, and a pair of fleece-lined leggings. After spending ten minutes primping in the bathroom mirror, I'm back with DeeDee.

One look at me and she asks, "Where are *WE* going?"

"Tariq...he wants me to meet him at Quigley Park."

Her searing gaze takes away my breath. "Right now? It'll be dark in less than an hour. Most Albuquerque parks at night are a big HELL NO."

"Yup."

Without asking, she leaves the couch and pockets her phone. "Let's go. Maybe we can be back before your mom. Drive or walk?"

I open the front door. "It's only up the street; we should leave your car here."

She closes the door behind us. "Good. I'm almost on 'e' anyway."

DeeDee tries to show me a reel, but between the fading Albuquerque sun and the sinking feeling I'm doing something wrong—just made everything right with my mom and now she doesn't even know I'm here!—my focus isn't the best.

"Samira's over there." She points. "That's your grandfather?"

I look past my BFF. "Yup, that's him. You want an introduction?"

Scanning the area, she says, "Nope. I'll find a place to sit."

"Be back."

"Okay."

The dry, brittle grass crunches under my feet. Tariq waits for me beside a single picnic table. His sunken cheeks are new. "Salaam, Leena. Thank you for coming. How about we go around the park two times?"

The slight breeze around is bearable. "Is your sister walking with us?"

She's still sitting in her SUV.

"No, Samira is here to make sure I don't overdo it. Again." He veers to the right. "Have you heard from Rheem? I had Samira give your number to her mother."

"Yeah, she texted me but I was at work and said I'd get back to her later."

His smile's even bigger.

120

"Alhamdulillah. With a little guidance from Rheem, you can work hard and get accepted into a top university."

His slow stride forces me to use smaller steps than normal.

"Mom says I shouldn't push myself too hard. She wants me to enjoy myself more, like going to a high school football game or maybe a dance. *Life is stressful enough* is one of her mottos."

I don't miss how his jaw tightens.

We're halfway around the park. As we approach a bench, I ask, "Do you need to rest?"

"No. Thank you for asking. Do you agree with your mom?"

Not knowing how much truth my grandfather can handle delays my words. But not wanting to offend him, I say, "Dancing isn't my thing and unless 'reading, then discussing fiction' becomes an Olympic sport, I'm not interested."

"So, you don't have a boyfriend?"

Flashes of anger swirl inside me. "No, I've never been on a date...but having the choice is more important than actually doing it."

My companion stops, then turns towards me. "Do you really believe that, or are those my daughter's words?"

Like I can't think for myself.

"Is it so bad to do normal teenage stuff? Is that what Islam teaches?" I dig my sneakers into the hard ground. "If it is, then I'm surprised more Muslim teens don't reject it."

Tariq shivers but he still manages to say, "It's not that simple, Leena. No matter what faith community a person is a part of, there are rules to follow." As we round the next corner, I catch him staring at me. "Today's youth don't understand that the One who created humanity knows what's best for us. Wanting a stable, happy marriage is what every parent wants for their children."

Small breaths escape my lips.

"How can anyone create a good marriage with someone they haven't ever kissed?" A voice inside me tells me to shut up, but I ignore it. "And why would anyone want to get married or even *think* about it while they're still in high school?"

"Our way of life is a protection against getting your heart broken, being taken advantage of, and ensuring no children are born to unwed parents. It's not a punishment, Leena."

And there it is—my very existence is problematic.

"Why would anyone want to make their life more difficult than it has to be? Don't worry, I'll get you a few books explaining the Muslim perspective on dating and marriage."

Before I can get my jumbled thoughts together and reply, his phone rings. "Salaam. No, Samira, we're both fine. InshaALLAH, I'll finish my walk then we can head home... wa alaykum as salaam."

We continue around the last half of the park, the silence only interrupted by the occasional car driving by.

"How often do you go walking?" Maybe asking a neutral question can save the situation.

He strides close enough that our elbows could touch.

"No more than twice a week, any more and my sister worries. But..." he whispers, "sometimes I walk circles in our backyard, to compensate for my love of cookies."

I feel the corners of my mouth rise into my first smile of our time together.

"Don't worry, your secret is safe with me."

We stop beside the picnic table where we met up. "InshaALLAH, we can talk again. Leena, please don't be offended by anything I said. That's not my intention."

His gentle voice convinces me he means it.

"Okay." But his words wounded me.

"Thanks for coming." He glances over his shoulder, probably making sure Aunt Samira isn't on her way to join us. "And I'll email you the information about Islam I promised you."

I wave, then watch as he walks away.

Are Tariq's steps even slower?

After scanning the park, I catch sight of DeeDee's cornrows at the bottom of the biggest playground slide. I'd bet a million dollars she's going to want to know everything. Time to come up with something good because I'm not sure what to tell her. And she can smell BS from a mile away.

But, when armed with the truth, DeeDee can come up with something good to tell my mom. "Sorry, if that took too long."

She waves away my apology. "Let's just get back to your house. I'm starving."

Each step on the hot sidewalk grows my dread.

"What's up? You look like someone stole your whole collection of fantasy books."

I glare at my BFF. "Don't even put that out there in the universe—what have my YA books ever done to you?"

DeeDee grins.

We head up the driveway, passing my mom's car.

I take short, deep breaths.

Before I can take my keys out of my back pocket, the front door swings open. "Welcome back."

The second after stepping into the house, all the delicious smells of our meal hit me.

Unfortunately, my mother is standing beside the kitchen table, her hands plastered on her hips. "So, who's explaining to me where you've been?" She points to her dinner haul. "Remember I just went out to get us food."

Not knowing what to say, my gaze lands on the floor.

The irritating beep of my bestie's notifications goes off. One look at her phone screen and she says, "Sorry, my tacos have to be to-go. I've been summoned home by Lilian."

My mom hands her a medium, brown paper bag dotted with grease stains.

"Thanks, Asiyah. Text me later, L."

Five seconds later, I'm facing the inquisition alone.

My mom sits. "You talk, I'll eat." After sliding me mine, she rips open her grease-stained paper bag.

After fishing out one of my tacos, I grab a big bite. My mouth fills with carne asada deliciousness. Out of the corner of my eye, I catch her glare on me.

"Tariq texted me and asked if I could meet him at Quigley Park, so we did."

She keeps eating her food. After finishing the first one, she says, "You didn't text me and let me know. Why the secrecy?"

I take a napkin from the middle of the table and wipe away some imaginary crumbs.

Here goes nothing.

"I just wanted to see him and didn't want to bother you with it." I breathe out super slow, hoping my lie is believable. Watching the sun's rays disappear from the table, my eyes move to the window. The last of the burnt-orange sky is on its way out.

The floor lamp tucked in the corner clicks on.

Damn automatic timer. I kinda wanted a few seconds of peace away from this situation.

My only living parent straightens her spine. "Then why all the secrecy?"

Memories of my never-shy mother telling off my fifth-grade teacher who didn't believe I didn't know anything about the maternal side of my family flashes across my mind.

I swallow my doubt. "You'll only make everything worse. My relationship with my grandfather is important to me."

The fury in her eyes could ignite a wildfire in this desert state. This shouldn't be happening.

"Leena, I get it. You're getting everything you've always wanted. But it's too much. When the hell will you wake up?" She pushes her food to the middle of the table.

Drops of regret fill my heart.

Did I make a mistake? Will I always have to choose a side?

"Mother, why is this so wrong? Today, it was just a walk in the park."

She sighs.

"It's never enough, daughter. You cater to them by going to Santa Fe and now this today. Is this how they expect you to behave? This is just the beginning. As nice as those two are being to you right now, things will change. They will change. You'll be expected to fulfill what THEY think—any independent dreams you have will be replaced if those two don't approve."

Her wide eyes haven't left my face.

A tiny piece of me wishes DeeDee hadn't left already—I need a witness.

It sucks my own mother believes I can't stand up for myself.

"This is pointless." She grabs a paper plate from the kitchen, then returns to the table and slides her open paper

126

bag of tacos onto it. "Make sure to leave the table as clean as you found it when you're finished."

She disappears behind her bedroom door.

Not fair—she hates it when I eat in my room. Looking around, the quiet I crave when the house is full of daycare kids is too much.

A tiny part of me knows DeeDee will know all the right things to say, like always, but I'm all talked out.

The starless night sky outside keeps me company as I nibble the rest of my food. Robbed of my joy, I sit here.

Alone. Emotional. Confused.

CHAPTER
FOURTEEN

January

After a full day of high school, I'm wrapped up in my blanket, trying to find the words to text Rheem back. *Either do or not*, that's what DeeDee would tell me.

> Hi, Rheem. It's Leena. Sorry it's been a minute—my daycare job is a lot.

> Hi! No problem. Is working with kids your thing?

She doesn't know how silly her question is.

> Nah. It's my mom's home-based business. But the money's good, for part-time work. No complaints. You work?

> Not anything regular—I babysit our neighbor's kids once a month. My parents want me to keep up my GPA, so I can get into a top college.

Damn. Her family too?

I forgot she's like a genius.

> But how do you get money??

Kinda personal for our first real conversation—oh well.

> In my house, good grades equal an allowance, and great grades equal a bigger allowance. ☺

That might motivate even me to find an academic passion. And then:

> Still interested in learning about Islam?

This could be a trick arranged by the Stewarts. But I'll bite.

> Yeah.

> My Islamic school is hosting a girls-only party. Wanna come?

I feel my eyes widen.

> Maybe. No boys allowed tho, rly?

Yes! This one's just for the girlies. We'll listen to music, do our nails…a henna artist might show up. AND tons of food and desserts 🎂

Sweets, huh? Well. Sugar is my favorite currency. But. I have to ask an obvious question.

Will I be the only non-Muslim girl there?

Don't know. Last time, there were 2 or 3. Does it matter?

I guess not!

I'd bet all the money I've ever earned at Asiyah's Angels that DeeDee will skip this one. No reason to ask.

Does Brother Tariq expect an Ivy League school? Is that why he wanted me to talk to you?

I jolt out of my bed.

You know…maybe? But what I want to study, no clue. If my grandfather expects the Ivies, he's going to be disappointed 🙁

> But you do want to go to college, right?

My fingers pause. That question hits a nerve.

> Not sure, tbh…My mother tells me to take my time. She'd rather I love my job than go after a ton of money 🤷

> I like that. Too many Muslim parents in our community expect one of three fields: Medicine, Law, or Engineering 👀

That sucks.

> Your parents too?

> Lucky for me, AND them lol, I want to study Biology. I already applied to five schools, early decision.

Damn. I'm not that girl.

> So when's the party?

> Saturday at 5, sorry for the short notice!! My mom can pick you up.

After our last conversation, I know my own mother wants *no part* of my plans to keep seeing anyone associated with the Stewarts. Especially a last-minute invitation to *this* kind of party.

> That's great if she could. Thank you!

> np! Just text me your address by Saturday morning, ok?

> Will do! 🖐

I squeeze my stuffed star. Both DeeDee and my mom always push me to be more social...but this won't impress them and failure is a real possibility.

But I'm doing it anyway.

"Leena, are you awake? We're going to Dion's!" Mom calls up.

"Coming!"

≈

Our booth is covered with a veggie pizza and huge family-sized Greek salad. I'm on my second slice when DeeDee tells us, "Guess what? I have another date with

Quan. We're going to Main Event this Saturday, with his cousin. Leena, you want to come?"

It takes me a minute, but I shake my head. I already have plans.

A strange air of tension wraps around us. They don't know about Rheem.

"You *should* go," my mom presses. "If I remember correctly, you like bowling!" She turns to my bestie. "And you need to make sure this guy isn't a loser."

I stuff my mouth with pizza, chewing each bite super slowly. Anything to give me time to think.

I keep my eyes on my plate, wondering what to do. Should I keep this a secret? *Can* I keep this a secret?

Only when my food is gone do I look up. Two pairs of eyes are glaring at me. The jig is up.

"I want to...but I have plans." I swallow hard. "I'm going to a girls-only party at the Islamic school. Rheem invited me."

"This meal is over," my mother says coldly. She heads to the counter for takeaway bags.

DeeDee stuffs another slice of pizza in her face before my mom returns and covers up the food. "Really, Leena? After what happened at the Islamic center's teen thing?"

"Rheem told me I'll be okay." With my eyes still fixed on DeeDee, I point at her. "Wait, Quan is taking you to an arcade? You never play any arcade games with me."

"I'm not planning on playing any with him either. But you have to give it to the dude. It's not the same boring date everyone else has at the skate park."

I think she *likes* this guy. "Just don't go to any escape rooms with him. That's our thing." Turning to my returning mom, I say, "Ma, you don't have to drive me on Saturday. Rheem's mom will pick me up."

"What about bringing you back home?" she hits back.

I forgot to ask, so I lie. "All taken care of!"

"Fine. *Fine*, then. Have fun."

My bestie pops out of her chair. "Well, I'm off to clean Lilian's house from top to bottom so she has nothing to say about my date." She winks at me. "Text me Saturday night or else. Good night!"

She leaves. With her gone, a tense silence settles.

"Mom," I venture, choosing my words carefully. "Why don't you have a guy in your life? Is it because you were raised as a Muslim? Tariq told me regular dating isn't allowed in Islam."

I see something in her eyes: pain. It hurts me.

"No, honey. Losing your dad before you were even born *crushed* me. Mateo was so kind and caring. We were sixteen, but we were in love. And after you arrived, I was way too busy working and taking care of you to find the energy for another relationship."

"What about now? I'm sixteen. Don't you think it's time?"

She waves away my question. "If I meet someone, that's great. But good men who would be okay with my crazy work schedule—and who are Michael B. Jordan–gorgeous—aren't that easy to find."

"That's a ridiculously impossible standard."

She finally smiles. "Guess I'm picky."

CHAPTER
FIFTEEN

January

When my eyes open the next morning, two flowy, long-sleeved shirts are resting on my desk. One's off-white with a high V-neck, the other light blue with a shimmer. I don't have to walk around with my bra on display, basically.

My mom comes through for me. I should've known she would.

One look at my phone and I hurry out of my room. It is *late*. 10:01 a.m.

"Good morning, sleepyhead!" My mom's at the kitchen table with a mug of her usual: full-caffeine coffee, three sugars. A half-eaten bagel sits on the plate in front of her.

"Morning. When did you get up? You didn't wake me?"

Her gaze moves to my face. "About an hour ago. Why should I wake you? We don't have any daycare kids today. Other than this Muslim thing, you have something else to do today?"

She did ask.

"No, nothing...DeeDee has her date, so...we didn't plan anything."

"Good. I'll be home doing a ton of daycare paperwork." I'd bet money I don't have she's playing hearts: Her face is already back into her screen.

Fine. Ten minutes later, I've eaten my cereal, loaded my dirty bowl and spoon into the dishwasher, and headed back to my room. After grabbing my backpack, I remove my math folder and dive in.

≈

"Leena, what are you doing?"

I stretch my legs out in front of me. "Homework."

"You've been doing that all day?"

"Well, I also went to the bathroom..."

"It's almost three o'clock; shouldn't you be getting ready?" She fills my doorway, her reading glasses perched on her nose.

"Yeah, you're right. I just need to take a shower and throw on my clothes." I point at the light blue shirt. "I'll wear that one. It goes best with my black jeans."

"What about makeup? Are you wearing any?"

My mom knows I don't own a single lipstick. Not really my thing. "Probably not."

She points over her shoulder. "If you change your mind, I put a couple things in the hallway bathroom."

"Really? Thanks." I shove my homework into my backpack, then stumble off my bed and into the bathroom. There's a brand-new eyeliner pencil and a sparkly lip gloss on the counter. The door's closed, but I hear her shout: "You're welcome! And use one of my perfume samples!"

I shower as fast as I can, the mirror fully fogged up by the time I'm done. I'm just getting out when my phone dings.

> Hi Leena! Be at your house by five

> We're going late, Rheem?

> Late? No such thing with a Musl m party. We'll be the first ones there.

I'm reminded how new all this is to me.

> Okay! I'm getting dressed 👗

Her thumbs-up emoji makes me smile, but then doubt creeps in. Is going really the right choice? Well. Even if it's not... it's too late to back out now.

I rush through my skincare routine, then apply the brown eyeliner and the lip gloss. Mom knew exactly what would look good on me—I guess because it looks good on her too. I dress, fix my hair, charge my phone, and by five, I'm pacing the living room.

The doorbell finally rings.

"I'll get it." My mom strides past me and yanks the front door open. "Hi, I'm Asiyah, Leena's mother."

Rheem is dressed in a puffer vest and all-black clothes, her skirt hem around her ankles. "Hello, ma'am, it's nice to meet you." She looks from Mom to me and back again, adjusting the scarf on her head, then asks me, "Do you have a curfew, Leena?"

I feel my eyes widen. *Curfew?* No one has ever asked this.

Mom jumps in. "My daughter just needs to text me before she leaves."

"I understand, Ms. Stewart. It was a pleasure meeting you." With Rheem leading the way, we head to a silver sedan and slip into the back seat together. My mom waves from the front door, then closes it.

Rashida turns her wide smile on me from the driver's seat. "Hello, Leena! How are you? I'm so glad you said yes to this. My daughter will make sure you have fun."

"Hello." Questions are flooding my brain, but I only whisper one to Rheem: "Are there going to be a lot of moms there?"

Shaking her head, she whispers back, "Maybe one or two… Don't worry. They spend the entire time talking together."

We smile at each other.

I know exactly what she means. It's just like a school dance.

Familiar streets pass by until we're in a neighborhood I've never seen before. Pulling up to an extra-large red brick building, the only way I know we're at the right place is the plain black-and-white sign above the door:

Al-Hidaayah Islamic School

Grades sixth through twelfth. We want our children learning it's okay to be both American and Muslim.

Rheem's mom points at the double doors. "My daughter will share with you how she *really* feels about this place during the party, when I'm not around."

"Mother, shouldn't we just go in?" Rheem asks, rolling her eyes.

Rashida turns off the ignition. I follow them through the school's double doors. The trophy case to the left of the entrance is full of ribbons and plaques. Too many. "Wow! Sports must be popular here."

Rheem's loud laugh echoes in the hallway. "Those trophies are all for academics."

My mouth wants to drop open, but I keep it closed. "Damn. Are *all* the students here overachievers?"

"Well...starting junior year, there are quarterly meetings with a college counselor. Senior year it's every month. So...perhaps!"

That's intense.

The three of us end up in the cafeteria—the healthy food posters give it away—but it's been transformed into a party space. Dark green and white streamers hang down the walls, with silver balloons covering half of the floor. Shimmery white fabric dresses each table. One whiff of the garlicky aroma of grilled meat, and I eagerly scan the room, finding the food table filled with at least four large, covered aluminum pans. My stomach gurgles.

But the sight *next* to the food makes saliva pool in my mouth. "What's that?"

Rheem stops beside me. "A candy bar—they have them at every one of these."

I've already spotted my favorite red licorice. DeeDee will never forgive me if I don't snag some for her too.

"Why the different-sized tables?"

Rheem doesn't even look. "The ones for two, those are henna stations. Later, you can get a design if you want. Ever had one? Do you know what it is?"

"It's like a hand tattoo, but...temporary?"

"You get it."

An older woman enters from a door in the back. She and Rashida embrace.

"Are we the only ones here?" This party isn't it.

"Don't worry," Rheem tells me. "Like I said, we're here first. By six, there'll be plenty of girls! Let's sit over there."

We snag seats at one of the big round tables in front of the candy.

"Leena," she begins, "when we met at your grandfather's house, I was pissed. I'm sorry about that. My parents made me cancel plans with my best friend to go to Santa Fe."

I feel the sides of my mouth turning up. "It's okay. My mom is a lot sometimes too."

"I hope we can be friends."

"Me too," I say, surprised to mean it. "What's your IG?"

We spend a happy half hour scrolling her stories. A stream of girls is starting to join us in the cafeteria, just like Rheem promised. I rub my sweaty palms down my lap. Even though most of them are wearing long black dresses, the range of colorful headscarves is a surprise.

Leaning over to Rheem, I whisper, "What's up with all the black?"

She scans them. "Those are abayas; they're like overcoats. You'll see their party clothes are underneath."

Worry hits me. "Party clothes? Am I underdressed?"

Her giggle doesn't reassure me at all. "Don't worry. You'll be fine."

As I catch some side-eyes from a few of the girls, I focus on Rheem instead of my peripheral. Besides, I have something new to ask. "Do you know Mo—I mean Muhammad Ameen?"

Shifting her chair closer to me, she says, "Yes, his family is well-known. His grandfather was one of the founders of the masjid." Rheem leans in, sharing my personal space, and lowers her voice to a murmur. "Why? You interested?"

"No! No...I'm just wondering. He's friends with an annoying guy from my school, so I kind of know him. And we spoke at the Muslim teen thing." I scan the room. "Why are we whispering?"

"He's a regular topic of conversation with most of the girls," she confides. "I mean, he's hot. But his traditional upbringing means he isn't interested in anything that isn't marriage."

That doesn't add up. "Isn't he still in high school? Aren't *they*?" I wish my mom had explained this to me. "Wait. Do *you* want to get married before you go to college?"

Now my companion sits up super straight. "We're not in that camp. But some families start looking once their daughters are close to finishing high school. It's a cultural thing."

Before I can ask any more, Rashida walks to the center of the room. "As-salaamu alaykum, everyone! As the PTO president, I'd like to welcome you all to our Teen Girl Night. No boys and no younger siblings were allowed, so each of you can enjoy yourselves."

Several girls clap and others yell, "Alhamdulillah!"

Rashida grins and, once the noise dies down, continues. "There's a room in the back for salaat. The henna artists and the female DJ have just arrived." Pointing to one of the back tables, she says, "Help yourselves to snacks and drinks. InshaALLAH, dinner will arrive in about an hour. Have fun!"

My new friend has shed her black abaya. Underneath, she's wearing sky-blue ribbed jeans and a yellow sweater with peek-a-boo shoulders.

"You look gorgeous!" I gasp.

She grins. "Thanks! Ready to eat?"

We head to the back and fill our plates up, then settle back in our seats. I have quite the haul: crackers, cheese cubes, olives, and a handful of strawberries and grapes.

Rheem's plate, however, has nothing on it I recognize. She's handing me what looks like a pizza pocket but much bigger. "Try a bite!"

I take it, but don't take a bite. "What is it?"

"Do you like beef?"

"Yes..."

"It's a meat pie—it's delicious."

After a long moment of thought, I sink my teeth into the pastry. The hint of garlic and an unfamiliar sweetness make this, easily, the best mouthful of my life. "WOW! I'm gonna need like a dozen more of those."

"Let me get you a few. Some of them have spinach inside, but I can tell the difference."

Rashida strolls over after Rheem leaves. "I'm glad you got some snacks. I want you to enjoy yourself tonight. Just let me know if you need anything."

"Thank you," I say, kinda embarrassed. Is this what being a Stewart is like...?

144

By the time her daughter is back with my meat pies, the female DJ is set up. I only have time to inhale one of them before a song blasts out of the speakers. Girls are coming out of their outerwear and unwrapping their hijabs, leaving piles of fabric on tables. I see everything from skintight dresses to crop tops to high-heeled boots. Everyone—me included—gets up. We're all dancing!

Some of the others have perfected the latest viral dance moves. *I've never been that on it.*

Rheem only sways from side to side, while I'm breaking a sweat grinding to the reggae beat. When the next song drops, my forehead and baby hairs are damp.

The dance floor fills up, but I'm pretty sweaty, so I reclaim my seat. A random girl brings me a water bottle—the coldness feels amazing in my hands. "Thanks," I say, surprised. She smiles without saying a word, then leaves.

I'm popping my last cheese cube in my mouth when Rheem joins me. "You're a good dancer," she says. It's such a casual comment, so clearly honest, that it really gives me a rare boost of confidence. After checking over her shoulder, Rheem admits, "I'm okay, but my mother pushes me to be more social. Starting to get a little socialized out. How are you doing?"

Wow. Sounds familiar. "I'm also okay, for now."

During the next two hours, the music only stops once. When it does, most of the girls, including Rheem, go into another room and pray. While they're gone, dinner arrives, and my stomach talks to me.

Rashida appears at the table again, startling me, a sweet smile still across her face. "Leena, please get some food. As our guest, you should go first. Don't be shy."

Rheem reappears before I can speak. "Follow me."

A step ahead, she leads me to the dinner line, explaining the things I don't recognize. "This salad, with the toasted pita bread on the top, is a must. And this, you gotta try this. It's grilled lamb and will go *fast*. And this hummus—after you taste it, you'll never eat that fake grocery-store stuff again." Without asking, she spoons some of it on my plate, which is fine with me because I love hummus.

We find our way back to the table. I scoop up a mouthful of the famous hummus with some pita bread. "Wow, that's delicious." The music is quieter, better for talking over, with lyrics in a language I don't understand. "Rheem...Do you like being a Muslim?"

My companion puts her fork down.

I hold my breath, crossing my fingers that the honest question didn't offend her. If it did, my grandfather will probably hear about it.

But a smile reappears on her face, and I exhale. "Since I was born into a Muslim family, that's what my parents passed down to me. I've never known anything else. The media always brings up the crazies but forgets to mention we're just like any other faith community."

"But...the no-dating thing...?"

"So? Do you date?"

"No, not yet—but I can if I want."

Rheem taps her chin. "So do we. There's a few in this room who have boyfriends their families don't know exist. Not me. Waiting until I'm married to have sex isn't that bad. Guys are supposed to wait, too, you know, it's not just the girls." She looks at me closely. "Wait. Are Brother Tariq and Sister Samira pressuring you to become a Muslim? 'Cause that's foul."

I sink lower in the hard plastic chair. "No, of course not." All of Samira's random statements and personal inquiries into my life run through my mind. "Do you think they would?"

The second after the question leaves my mouth, I want it back.

She shrugs, then points to one of the smaller tables. "The line's gone! We can get some henna! Let's go."

I follow her.

The henna artist is wearing a red sweatshirt and matching hijab. "Salaam, Rheem. Who's your friend?"

"Wa alaykum as salaam, Iya—this is Leena."

I return Iya's teeth-baring smile. "Hi. Does getting one of these hurt?" Pain and I aren't friends.

"Don't worry; other than the paste being a little cold, nothing will hurt." Iya points to the postcard on the table. "Check out my page to see more of the designs I've done."

Rheem lays her palm in front of Iya. "I'll go first. A big flower with lots of details, please."

"Your usual? Got it!" She cleans Rheem's palm and the inside of her wrist with an alcohol wipe, then picks up a clear plastic cone with a deep greenish liquid inside. Then she draws a circle on my first Muslim friend's skin. With her magic, a flower slowly and perfectly takes shape.

"That's amazing," I admit. "You're so talented. Do you draw all your designs freehand?"

Without lifting her gaze up, Iya says, "I work best like that, but if someone really wants something specific, I'll try to copy it."

A familiar song escapes the speakers. None of the chaperones react to the sexy lyrics. I heard from DeeDee our principal refused to allow this song to be played at *our* last school dance. No need to share that.

"What do you think?" Rheem holds her arm up; the henna flower and its petals cover her entire palm and trail down her forearm.

It snatches my breath away. "So beautiful."

"Would you like one?" Iya asks, raising an eyebrow.

"I...yes." Having a reminder of tonight, I think, is a good idea. "Can you do something simple, like ivy?"

Iya smiles. "Yes."

While she's working, I turn to Rheem. "You can hang out with your friends, if you want. I'm okay here."

Her face drops. She looks away.

A minute later, she reveals in a hushed tone, "My besties aren't actually here. Our trio isn't much into hanging with most of these girls."

I realize that, if it wasn't for me, she wouldn't even be here. "No, I get it. This is fun, but dances aren't really my thing either. I came for you. Because you invited me. And I appreciated that, Rheem."

She rewards me with a wide grin.

~

The rest of the night flies by. My dark henna paste dries, and I finish every bite of food on my plate. On the ride home, Rheem shares some links with me of colleges that have strong creative writing programs. "Since you're addicted to reading, maybe you should consider writing your own stories."

I shake my head. "I'm no Sabaa Tahir or Tracy Deonn."

She pinches my arm. "But you never *know*."

Maybe. I sink into my seat and try to imagine books that other people will read. Her unfounded confidence in me is special, and completely crazy.

As we pull up into the driveway, Rashida speaks to me. "I hope you had fun, Leena?"

"I did. Thank you for including me." Turning to her daughter, I say, "And thank you too."

"Don't be a stranger, girl. You promised me some book recs."

I get out of their sedan, holding my take-home plate of food and my bag full of licorice. Rheem and I wave at each other until I lose sight of them.

Admitting to my mom that I had a good time is not going to be easy.

I'm not sure how she'll take it—but maybe she's already asleep.

No. The second I'm behind the front door, I know my luck has run out. My mom is parked on the couch, her nose in this month's issue of Albuquerque *Local*. "So, how was it?"

I step out of my shoes, very slowly.

"That bad?" she asks.

Once the extra plate is stashed in our fridge, I shuffle back into the living room, stopping beside the couch. "No. Honestly, it was great. We danced, ate lots of delicious food..." I hold out my palm. "Look at my henna."

Her neutral expression doesn't budge. "Nice. No one said anything rude to you, really?"

My spine straightens. "No one."

She closes her magazine, stands, and walks out. "I'm glad. Of course, when my family finds out, they'll use this to their advantage."

"Why can't you just be happy for me?" Smothering anger chokes me. "Aren't you always pushing me to, and I quote, 'expand my social circle'? Now that I am, it's still a problem."

"It's a problem that you think you're an expert on the dysfunctional Stewart family."

"Seriously?" I throw my arms up. "Just because *you* chose to cut them off doesn't mean *I* have to. Seems to me that all *three* of you are part of the problem, and the only one who suffered from it was me!"

With that little pearl of wisdom, I fast-walk into my room, then slam the door so hard that a couple novels on my bookshelf fall out.

Damn.

This isn't what I've always wanted.

CHAPTER
SIXTEEN

January

I'm deep into a bowl of cereal when the doorbell rings. Which, wild, since the digital microwave clock shows 7:15.

My mom leaves the kitchen, skirting by the table where I and her untouched mug of coffee sit. "Maybe DeeDee forgot her key." She peeks out the peephole. "What the *hell*?"

"Ma, who is it?"

She yanks the door open. "*What are you doing here?*" Her sharp, accusatory tone catches my attention.

"I missed you. How are you? How's business?"

I strain to catch a glimpse of the owner of the deep baritone voice, but my line of sight is blocked.

My mom steps outside without a coat, in just her Asiyah's Angels work polo and jeans, and shuts the door behind her. I can hear a quarrel, but nothing concrete.

I *want* to sneak closer to the front door, but I don't. When Ma finally comes back inside our little house, my eyes follow her every move. She rewarms her coffee, then sits across from me, not once meeting my gaze.

Am I really going to have to *ask* who that was?

"Look, you probably have questions, I get that." Her voice shakes, an unfamiliar sound. "Give me a second."

The air around us feels thinner—harder to breathe. And the light streaming in from the front window offers no comfort.

"His name is Robert. We used to date. He just *showed up*, unannounced." She raises her head. "Don't worry. I told him not to come back unless he's invited."

Her confession shocks my nervous system. "Date?! You're telling me you had a secret boyfriend? Where the hell was I?"

Her phone alarm interrupts our conversation. The first daycare kids will be here in fifteen minutes. And where's DeeDee? It's Monday, and we have to get going soon. She hates being late to first period.

After swiping her alarm off, my mom takes a long, deliberate sip. "I met Rob right before you finished eighth grade. We dated for a few years, but it wasn't anything serious. I was busy with the daycare, and eventually he complained about it—so the relationship died last summer. No reason to tell you after that."

Her ridiculous excuses are BS. "A couple of *years*? Last *summer*? You told me there was never a man in your life after Dad. You're full of secrets! First, Tariq and Samira—now this!" I scoot my chair back, giving her my best glare. "Next I'll find out the two of you have a secret child. Maybe I've got a sibling out there somewhere."

"Leena, you have every right to be upset, but freaking out doesn't help anyone." Her calm words can't hide a touch of panic in her eyes. "Yes, I've hidden big things from you, but a pregnancy isn't one of them. Now please calm down—the daycare families will be arriving soon."

Who is this person in front of me?

"You should've invited homeboy in. My whole thing right now is meeting people I didn't know were in your life." I shake with pent-up anger I'm barely holding in.

A text notification erupts. Ma glances at her screen and back at me. "Deidre had a flat tire. She should be here by eight."

"You've been lying to me my entire life!"

My mom stands. "We need to postpone this conversation until later. You have school, and I have to take care of other people's children. Please pretend you don't hate my guts for the day."

"Hey, are you going to explain what's going on? You and your mom didn't exchange two sentences when we got home." DeeDee sits crisscross on one end of the bed, and I sit at the other, leaning against the wall and squeezing my pillow. My stomach rumbles, reminding me I skipped lunch.

"This morning, a guy Ma used to date stopped by."

Her mouth drops. "No shit? Date?!"

"Even my imagination couldn't make this drama up." My gaze drops. "It's like my entire life is an illusion. My mom has been keeping so, so much from me. It's kind of scary."

"Well, okay, what did she say about the guy? She had to explain it to you, right?" DeeDee always believes the best about my mom. Just once, I wish she'd share my anger.

"His name is Robert. She said they dated for *years* and only broke it off *last summer.* Apparently, he couldn't deal with how much time Asiyah's Angels took up, and they broke up. Who knows."

My bestie checks her phone. "It's Lilian. Girl, I gotta head out. Don't take it personal; maybe she wanted to protect you." She stretches, then leaps up.

I whisper, "Bye," but she's already gone. Before I can lose myself in my English homework, my phone rings.

"Tariq!"

"Salaam, Leena. How are you?"

I lie. "I'm great."

"Alhamdulillah. Are you free this Wednesday night? I'd like you to come have dinner with us."

It takes me a minute to decide. "Sure, I'd love to...but it's a school night, so if we could have an early meal, I'd really appreciate it. Would you like me to bring something?"

His chuckle brings a small smile to my face. "That's not necessary. InshaALLAH, it will just be the three of us. There's something I want to discuss with you, and I promise, we'll make sure you're home at a reasonable time."

"Oh . . . okay, then."

"See you soon. Salaam."

"Bye!"

Something I want to discuss with you . . . My mind's racing with a million possibilities. Before this morning, I might have considered telling my mother about this mysterious sentence—but forget that. She's not the only one who can have secrets.

≈

"Leena, make sure to put away the crayons when those two are done coloring," my mom reminds me, pointing at the box on the floor. "Spending an hour scrubbing walls isn't something you want to do tonight."

She's acting like my dinner plans don't exist.

"Ma, remember, I'm visiting Tariq and Samira tonight." The overly sweet tone in my voice won't fool her. She can sense the anger I'm holding in.

She keeps her voice mild. "Make sure you take your keys with you. I've got plans, too, and don't want you to get locked out."

This is new. But I don't comment. "So, do I have to be home by a certain time?"

"Just text me if you won't be home by ten p.m. And no need to wait up for me."

If this is our new mother-daughter normal, it sucks.

By the time Samira has picked me up and driven me most of the way to my grandfather's house, I'm super pissed. (Not that my aunt notices. She's deep into the Motown songs streaming through the speakers.)

"Sister Rashida told me you had a good time at the Al-Hidaayah teen party. Is that true?"

Weird question. Why would Rheem's mom lie? Using my unnaturally sugary-sweet voice again, I say, "Yes, it was so fun. The music was great, the food was amazing."

We're in the Las Campanas neighborhood now, and I take in all the massive homes and snow-dusted yards. Teens around here all probably have their own cars.

When we pull into my grandfather's impressive circular driveway, my stomach knots. If he wanted to talk about something simple, wouldn't he have just called me on the phone?

I follow my aunt inside the house. "Don't forget to take off your shoes. InshaALLAH, we're having dinner in the dining room."

I slip out of my scuffed sneakers and leave them on the shoe rack beside the front door. As we enter the kitchen, the garlicky aroma of grilled meat hits my nose.

"InshaALLAH, you're hungry, because I've been cooking all day." Aunt Samira points towards the sparkling countertops. "Had to clean for close to an hour before I left to pick you up."

Had to? Should I say thank you?

"Salaam, Leena. Thank you for joining us." Tariq appears and walks towards us, a wide smile taking over his face. "How are you?"

I return his smile...but his stride is slower than the last time I was here, and he's swimming in his button-down shirt. He doesn't look well at all.

"Great! Good! Nothing's changed. Still going to school and working at the daycare." I point in a random direction. "Is that the way to the dining room? Shall we?" I want my grandfather to sit down right away.

Aunt Samira sighs. "Tariq will show you to the dining room. I'll bring in the food."

We head down a large hallway, my sock-covered feet sinking into the plush carpet runner. My grandfather opens a set of double doors. "Here we are."

It's not just the long, solid wood table with eight chairs that snatches away my breath.

It's the black two-level chandelier (which probably costs more than Ma earns all year). It's the slight cinnamon scent—subtle, classy. It's the table settings, all burgundy linen and gold dishware. It's the cream tablecloth, with its decorative swirls and embroidered lace border (I'm reminded of one of my favorite YA fantasy's court scenes).

"Wow. Do you eat in here *every day*?"

He shakes his head. "My sister decorated it. Other than the month of Ramadan, it's only used for her meals with her friends."

A strange question pops into my brain, and after checking it's still just the two of us, I lean in. "Do you or Samira have any non-Muslim friends?"

His expression betrays nothing. Damn. Is that even okay to ask?

Turns out, it is. "I've been involved in interfaith work for many years. I'm fortunate to count several people from other faith communities as friends. We've had them over for dinner many times."

My aunt enters the room, carrying two white platters. I rush in her direction. "Let me help you." I hold out my hands.

Wouldn't want my aunt to think I don't have home training.

Samira passes them to me and heads back into the kitchen. We do this dance a couple of times. Finally, the three of us are seated around a table groaning with food. "Help yourself, Leena. My sister is a terrific cook, as you know. Do you like lamb?"

It takes me a second to remember the last time I had it. "Yeah."

Samira loads a small chop on my dinner plate, following it up with asparagus and half a spoon of potatoes. She gives each of us a small dollop of salad on a side plate and a glass mug of hot tea. When my dinner companions put their fabric napkins across their laps, I do it too.

I take a taste of everything I'm given. "This salad is delicious—what's in it?" I ask. "We don't eat a lot of greens at home."

"It's spinach, heirloom tomatoes, and English cucumbers. I topped it with Parmesan cheese shavings and a simple vinaigrette." Her voice is a little tart. "You can take some home if you like. Show your mother. Maybe she'll make it for you."

Tariq's dinner is only half-eaten, but his salad, at least, is history. "Now, Leena, you're probably curious about what we wanted to discuss with you. It's something positive, I promise."

"Okay." My back dampens.

"Both Samira and I think you should consider moving in here with us."

Is...he serious?

The shock mutes me. All I can do is stare.

"Please consider it. Living with us would allow you to attend the best public school in the state for your final two years. Their graduation rate and four-year college acceptance rate is close to ninety percent and close to half of the students take AP classes. InshaALLAH, with hard work, you could get accepted into any university you applied to!"

The setting winter sun is almost gone. The room darkens enough for me to squint. Samira leaves the table, flicks on the chandelier, and comes right back.

"Would...I...have to become a Muslim?" My mouth is dry, but I push the question out. It has to be asked.

The Stewarts across the fancy table from me aren't smiling anymore.

"Leena, accepting Islam isn't something that should be forced. It doesn't work that way." Tariq's tone is all business. "It's a *very* personal decision."

Aunt Samira clears her throat. "But we would expect you to adhere to certain rules. You'd have a curfew, you'd be expected to get top grades, and you'd go to college right after high school. Those are requirements." There's a sharp tinge to her voice. These are the *do's*, but I can tell they've also come up with a list of *don'ts*.

My mind wanders, panic setting in. How the hell can they think leaving my mom is an option?

My grandfather's eyes bore into mine. "Please. Say something."

I down a swig of warm tea, stalling. "What about Mom? She'd be alone."

"You could still work at the daycare during the summer," Samira offers, unenthusiastically.

"You'd need a car—something reliable. Of course, we'd make sure you have that."

"I'll have to get my license first," I say with little enthusiasm.

Deserting my only living parent isn't something I'm going to do. Yeah, we're not in the best place right now, but that part of Stewart family history shouldn't be repeated.

And yet...that's what they're asking me to do. Repeat history.

Was my mom right about these people?

"Leena, we know this is out of the blue and a huge decision. But we only want what's best for your future." My grandfather reaches for my hand. His is dry, scaly, sick-feeling.

"Then you'll understand that I need to think about it, before I ever bring it up to my mom." My voice is hoarse. "Thank you for offering."

Samira leaves the room, without saying anything to anyone.

"InshaALLAH, take all the time you need. There's just over four months until the school year ends." My grandfather stands. "I'll have my sister put together some leftovers for you to take."

He didn't ask if I'm ready to go, but I am. He leaves me in the cavernous dining room.

The extended family I've dreamed of for my entire life is actually a nightmare. It's forcing me into some seriously messed-up situations.

I hear raised voices in the plush hallway. I cover my ears, hoping they're not arguing about me, but knowing they are. Samira reappears in the doorway of the dining room. "InshaALLAH, after maghrib, I'll drive you home."

I'm too young for all this.

CHAPTER
SEVENTEEN

January

"You look good, almost like normal," I tell DeeDee. "How do you feel?"

She plops down in the chair closest to me. "Better. Having a 102-degree fever sucks. Kept falling asleep watching Netflix."

My secret (AKA the uncomfortable, life-changing, bizarro invitation to live with my grandfather) is the only thing I've thought about for two days. Maybe I can tell her now that she's recovered from the flu.

"Good evening, Deidre." My mom joins us at the table. "I hope, since you're here, that you're no longer sick."

Damn. I push the secret further down inside me.

"No more body aches and my cough is almost history. How about we all have Blake's to celebrate?"

"You two enjoy. I have dinner plans." My mom's cryptic answer pushes all my buttons. I turn around to give her a closer look. She's wearing a curve-hugging burgundy sweater dress, her shoulder-length hair curled, her face full of makeup.

It's a random Friday night—her behavior is suspect.

"Have fun," DeeDee tells her, as if there's nothing concerning happening.

She leaves us. I peek out of a living room window as she backs out of the driveway and drives down the street. If *I* left the house without telling her *my* plans, there'd be hell to pay.

"My mom is too much," I mutter. "Okay, girl, we NEED to talk. Blake's is on me."

DeeDee smacks the table. "Oooh, you offering to pay? It must be something juicy!" She grabs my phone. "I'll do the order. What do you want?"

Ten minutes later, we're facing each other on the couch, a bag of Sour Patch Kids candy on the cushion between us (a light pre-dinner snack, as one does).

"Okay, spill it."

"I had dinner with the Stewarts on Wednesday. While we were eating, Tariq asked me...to move in." I tried to sound deliberate, emotionless. But I probably didn't hide how much saying it to another person freaks me out.

"He did? That's *crazy*." My bestie reaches over and shoves my shoulder. "And Samira is okay with this? How did they react when you said no?"

Her eyes widen as I bite my bottom lip, not saying a thing.

"Wait...are you actually considering it?"

The room darkens with evening. I catch a glimpse of cotton-candy skies out the window. The table lamp next to me turns on. Damn timers.

"No. I'm not. Not really. But there's a part of me that's curious... I mean, something's going on with my mom. It's really uncomfortable here." I swallow my nervousness.

"What about her feelings?"

I take a minute to respond. "No, I know. My grandfather thinks going to a better high school will give me a better chance of getting into a top university, but I—"

She snaps her fingers inches from my face. "You don't even know if you want to go to college. What about our plans after graduation? I bet those would disappear. Without a roommate, I'd have to keep living with Lilian!" She's getting loud. "You'd be doing that to me!"

A notification interrupts us. "Food's here."

She heads to the front door, opens it, and accepts a large bag from the delivery guy. "Thanks."

We resume our seats, at least now with delicious food. I sink my teeth into my chicken burger. "This ranch sauce is my favorite."

DeeDee grimaces. "You'd really be okay with leaving this house? You grew up here."

"I'm not okay with it. I think it was wrong for them to even ask. But I guess... I guess I want the chance to consider it, after all."

"Also: telling your mom about this completely inappropriate offer from them. Any ideas about how you're doing that?"

166

The chicken becomes a lead weight in my stomach. "Got no clue."

≈

"So," DeeDee announces the next morning, after staying the night, "it only happens once or twice a year, but Lily actually gave me money this week."

DeeDee's grandmother is a special one. "She what now?"

"She won at blackjack and had a moment of weakness." Her big smile is beautiful. "So I'm taking us to Santa Fe."

"Santa Fe? *That's* where we're going?"

She looks me right in the eyes for a split second, then returns her gaze to the road. "If my bestie is going to be living there, we need a few new places to go. Like this cute little patisserie shop I have in mind. You'll see!"

It takes us an hour (we burn time singing along to playlists), but we finally reach snowy St. Francis Drive. Ten minutes later, we pull into a parking lot in a commercial area.

"Are you sure this is it?" My hand is on the door handle.

DeeDee grabs her tote bag. "Yup. This is Lilian's favorite bakery. Sometimes she'll drive up here to get her favorite raspberry croissants. When I was, like, eight or nine, we came together."

To me, the building looks like a manufactured home, but the sign tells us we're in the right place. As we enter, the air smells like melted butter and cinnamon. I take in a big breath.

"Hi, how many for breakfast?" an older lady asks, smiling, behind the hostess podium. Her large turquoise pendant hanging off a thick silver chain is a little much for 9 a.m.

"Just the two of us." DeeDee points to an empty booth. "We'd like to sit there."

The hostess nods. "This way."

Once we're settled into our seats, I study the breakfast options. "Girl, do you see these prices? Their breakfast burrito is *sixteen* dollars."

She just nods. "Black. Jack. Winnings." When the waiter appears, she says, without hesitation, "I'm having the green chili quiche. L?"

"A breakfast sandwich," I manage, even though I'm still nervous about the cost, "with veggie bacon."

My bestie is studying the menu again. "And two semi-sweet hot chocolates."

"Those are great." He takes our menus. "I'll be back soon."

My eyes scan the dining room. There isn't another Black person here—worse, a blonde woman directly across from us keeps eyeing me.

"Girlie, what are you looking at?" DeeDee asks.

I lean closer to the table. "Someone thinks we're interesting." I shift my eyes to my right.

DeeDee turns her entire body to face the lady. Thirty seconds of intense stare-down ends when homegirl at the other table finally looks away. A minute later, Blondie and the guy with her get up and leave.

"Some of these bougie Santa Fe people are too much!"

"You think I'd always get that kind of reaction if I moved here?" I ask.

She shrugs. "If you asked your aunt or your grandfather, would they tell you the truth?"

I have no idea. "Maybe that lady was just a rude tourist. It's the oldest state capital in the country. They're always around."

"Maybe. Maybe not. Some rich folks don't like us too close. The median home price here is like two hundred thousand dollars higher than Albuquerque."

My mouth falls open.

"What? Now that my bestie is related to money, I got curious. Google is right here." She pats the phone in front of her. "If you live with the Stewarts, these menu prices would be affordable."

She is too much.

"Don't even go there," I say. "Me and you are together in the struggle."

She lays her white paper napkin across her lap but doesn't say a word.

Money could never come between a sisterlike friendship. We wouldn't let it because we're too close for that. Right?

The waiter is back. "Here you go. Please be careful; these plates are hot. Enjoy."

I dive right in. It's heavenly. By the time my stomach is full, I still have half of my order; the portions were so generous. When I check out DeeDee's situation, it's the same. Our server brings us the bill and two to-go boxes. Once we're paid up, my bestie gets a slice of carrot cake for the road.

The ride back is much quieter. Between the sugar and the car heater on full blast, my eyelids get heavy....

"Hey, wake up, sleepyhead!" She shakes my shoulder. "Have a good nap?"

I rub my eyes. "Sorry." Now that we're back in Bernalillo County, my pulse is racing. "Should I tell my mom what we did today?"

She cracks her gum. "You need to start with dinner at your grandfather's."

I pick at my cuticles the rest of the way home.

As we pull into the driveway, I ask, "You're coming in, right?"

"Sure," she says. "I have to go to the bathroom anyway."

With my to-go box in hand, I step out of the car into a sudden cold breeze. We step through the front door to see that my mom has her utility bills spread out on the kitchen table. "Hey, you two. How was your day?"

Without a single sound, my BFF heads to the toilet.

"Ma...there's something we need to talk about." My words come out a whisper, but I push through. "Tariq and Samira asked me if I'd consider living with them."

Mom's lips flatten. "Excuse me? What *possible* reason did they give to justify that? It's fucking *ridiculous*."

My thoughts are a jumbled mess. "He wants me to attend a high school in Santa Fe; he said it's ranked top in the state. He said it would help me get into a good college. It's...it's nothing against you."

"Ha! Really? You've only been in their lives for a couple of months. What's their rush?" She rises, a deep frown creasing her pretty face. "Why is it okay for them to plan your future? I think it's because they couldn't do it to me—they want another bite at the apple. And another thing! As your legal guardian, you need my permission. If I don't agree, are they taking me to court?"

"You're not...you're not willing to even discuss it with them?"

Her glare hardens. "This shit is crazy. Is this my punishment for leaving when I was a teenager? Luring my child away is *low*." She keeps her eyes pinned on me. "I can't do this right now." She grabs her phone, house keys, and sneakers. "I need a few minutes."

She hurries out the front door.

So. Tonight is ruined.

My bestie reappears, pulls me into my bedroom, and shuts the door. "L, are you going to be all right? Your mom was super pissed—the walls are *thin* in this place."

I shrug, shaken, and continue to pick at my cuticles. They're starting to bleed. "Do I think my life is in danger? No. But I expect more mess."

DeeDee puts a hand on my arm. "I'll stay again if you want."

She really is the only reason I'm surviving lately.

"Thanks, but that's not necessary. We don't *both* have to be in her sights." I gift her a weak smile. "But please, please keep your phone on. If you get an SOS from me, will you come back?"

"Will do."

≋

A loud knock.

"Yes?"

My mom barges in. She pulls out my desk chair, sets it in front of me, and plops down into it. "Still thinking of moving out?"

"It isn't my idea! I'm just curious. *Curious.* I actually think it was wrong for them to..."

Our eyes meet. The fiery intensity of her stare might burn me. "Let me ask you: Do they expect you to become a Muslim?"

Same question I asked. I am my mother's daughter.

"Tariq told me something as big as that would be my decision."

"Yeah, right." She leans back, her arms across her chest. "I don't care what he said. I'd bet money that's his ulterior motive. It's Samira's for sure."

"Maybe. Please, Ma, help me understand this thing. Can you see anything positive about their offer?"

"Nope. Funny, you never told me it's your dream to go to an Ivy after graduation. Or is that *his* idea?" She snaps in the air between us. "Look, if either one of them was that worried about your education, there are private schools *here* you could attend that would take their money. This offer is about *having control*. Been there, lived that."

I'm confused. "We just met. Why do they want to control me?"

She claps twice. "Exactly. You just met. Why do those two think they know what's best for you? What gives them the right to an opinion? It's not *about* you, Leena. It's about me. Me, and them, and my mom."

"Ma, are you talking about now, or when you were my age?"

Her face morphs.

Little by little, the hard edges of her expression disappear, replaced by a total poker face. "I can't make this decision for you. Don't rush it." Her voice softens. "And don't let anyone influence you, either way. Not even me. I know how that feels and it's horrible. That's enough for now. I'll yell when dinner is ready."

Alone again.

I curl up on my bed and stare at the ceiling. Waiting for answers to questions I've only ever asked myself.

An email notification pops up on my phone. I reach over.

Good Afternoon Leena,

How are you today? I hope you're thinking about our offer. Please know it's not just me—Samira agrees it would be a great thing.

Yes, my sister and my daughter aren't on good terms.

But know this: Samira has experienced loss in her life. And Samira gave up everything to come and live with us when your grandmother died.

In time, I hope you will recognize her many positive qualities.

Have you mentioned this offer to your mother? I love Asiyah, but with our difficult past, it wouldn't surprise me if she tries to dictate your choice. InshaALLAH, my intention is just to help you get the best education possible! My only grandchild shouldn't have to suffer because her family is fractured.

Maybe it's selfish of me to want to spend even more time with you. But you're a special young lady, and I'd be honored to help you achieve all your worldly dreams.

Let me know if you want to discuss anything—or just stop by for a visit.

Your loving grandfather,

Tariq Stewart

My eyes stay stuck on the screen for a long time.

Slowly, a spark of courage forms inside me. So what if she refuses to talk about it? Screw it. If I don't ask, I'll never have the chance to know.

With my phone in my back pocket, I'm up on my feet. As I enter the kitchen, my mom lays a tray of homemade nachos on the top of the stove. "Good, you're here. It's almost dinnertime."

"Ma, I have to show you something." I hand her my phone.

"What's this?" Her gaze moves slowly over my grandfather's email. Without a single comment, she hands me back my cell.

"You have nothing to say?"

"Let's eat first."

We do. I watch her, but she never once locks eyes with me. My plate is almost empty when she speaks again.

"I'm not surprised by anything he said. My dad always has the best intentions, or so he says. But his bank balance and the high educational goals he pushed on me didn't replace my grief, and ultimately, they didn't help me either."

175

I try to choose my next question wisely. "What...what kind of loss did Samira suffer?" Should be safe enough to start.

My mom stares out the window. "Samira got married when I was ten. Less than two years later, her husband died suddenly."

"That's terrible."

"So...when my mom died...your grandfather thought by having her come live with us, we'd all heal from our losses together." She downs her water. "Only, Samira thought my mom was too lenient with me and convinced my dad I needed more structure—more rules."

I get it now. "And you doubt she's changed."

We polish off dinner. It takes me a while to ask what I really want to ask. "After you had me...why did you stay away from them?"

Her eyes find mine, surprisingly sad. "I knew most of the parents of my Muslim friends wouldn't want their daughters around me. I didn't finish high school and had a baby without a husband—a bad influence."

"Maybe you were wrong? Tariq doesn't seem like he's that judgmental."

Her pursed lips tell me I'm wrong. "When Samira first found out about my friendship with your dad, she told me if I 'disgraced the family' and had a relationship outside of marriage, she and Tariq would marry me off to the first eligible Muslim brother they could find."

"Wait, *what?*"

"Rehashing all of this isn't helping either of us." She glances at her plate in disgust. "I just want to let the past go. But...if we're being very honest, I have something to tell you too. I've reconnected with one of my friends from years ago, and we've been hanging out. Tonight, Carla is dragging me to a comedy club downtown."

"Oh! It's a friend! I thought...Well, thanks for telling me where you've been going."

Her smile brings out one of my own. "I can't expect you to be honest with me and keep secrets from you. I suppose I felt a little protective of my new social life; it's been so long since I had one. Leena?"

"Yes?"

"I'm sorry. I made what I thought were the best decisions."

I reach out my hand and she grabs it. "Thanks for saying that. Ma, I'm not unhappy with our life here. But sometimes...Well, it would've been nice to have *family*. Like at Christmas and Easter."

"Sorry, kid, those are Christian holidays. The Stewarts don't celebrate them."

"Oh. Okay. But you know having people at my elementary and middle school graduations was something I always wanted. No—it's not about the graduations. It's about people. Just people. In general. To support me. To support *us*." My mom's openness tonight is a gift I didn't expect, so I leave it there. "Now go have fun with your friend."

CHAPTER
EIGHTEEN
February

"Leena, wake up!"

The pounding on my door forces my eyes open. "DeeDee...?"

Seconds later, she's sitting on the edge of my bed.

"What?" I sit up. "It's way too early to be awake on a Saturday. Did we have plans today?"

My BFF drops a flyer in my lap.

After scanning it, I jump up. "Give me ten minutes to shower and get dressed. Get two reusable bags from the kitchen; we're going to need them to carry our books."

She winks at me. "Already done. Couldn't let you miss the main library's semiannual sale."

By the time I'm ready in a plaid miniskirt, fleece-lined leggings, and navy sweater, my mom is up, nursing a cup of coffee. I must have forgotten to add Feb. 17th to my Google calendar.

"Good morning."

"Ma, is it okay that we go out?" Maybe I should've asked first.

Her full smile is a good sign.

"Deidre already told me the plans. I can handle the two toddlers coming today. Have fun." She waves. "Remember to leave some YA fantasy for other people."

We head out and get in DeeDee's car.

"No way."

I fasten my seat belt and pick up a white to-go bag. "What's this?"

"Two Java Joe's breakfast burritos. Mine with red chili, yours with salsa." After reaching into the back seat, she hands me a drink. "Here's your chai latte."

I take a quick sip of my favorite beverage. "What did I do to deserve all this pampering?"

She backs out of the driveway and heads down the street. "Part of a BFF's job."

I don't deserve her.

"So, how was it?"

Time to come clean. "At first, very tense. Then she told me, after her mom died, Samira moved in with them. They didn't get along since my aunt is much stricter when it comes to all things religion. I guess my grandfather sided with his sister."

"Damn, that must've been rough." She's an expert on difficult family members.

I nod. "You know the rest. My mom ran away from home—going almost seventeen years without seeing either Tariq or Samira."

We ride along, listening to my bestie's favorite playlist.

But by the time DeeDee parks, my burrito is half-gone. Ten minutes later, we're both stuffed and ready to shop. The basement room is filled with tables and tables of books ranging from fifty cents to five dollars.

"Good morning and welcome," a gray-haired woman welcomes us. "Let me know if you need any help."

I scan the room, my gaze landing on the fantasy section. "Thanks."

My BFF points to the reference section. "I'll be over there."

I'm deep into deciding between two newer young adult titles, when I hear, "Wow, I've been waving for at least five minutes and nothing. You really didn't see me?"

The deep voice is one I recognize. "Hi! Mo!"

He's carrying a full paper bag. "Hey. So, you're a reader too?"

"Nothing is more important to me than my fantasy collection." I lean closer, trying to see his books. "What you got?"

Muhammad sifts the bag to his other hand. "A couple coffee table books for my parents, one on world architecture and one on Islam. The rest are professional athlete biographies."

Does my breath reek of salsa? "Are you here by yourself?"

Even his laugh is adorable. "Yup. Books aren't exactly Ray's favorite things."

Why they're best friends, I'll never understand. A question pops into my head. "Did you get in trouble for talking to me at the Muslim teen event?"

My heart is racing, but his warm smile hasn't changed. "No. Some brother saw us together and told my dad, but he knows I'm trustworthy. And as the youngest of five kids, my siblings would all gang up on me if I even thought about playing with a girl's emotions."

There's a kaleidoscope of butterflies dancing in my stomach. "That's good to know. When Samira told me your dad spoke to my grandfather, I thought the worst."

We step to the opposite side of the fantasy table.

"Don't worry about that. Brother Tariq is a respected elder. My dad probably wanted to make sure he knew we weren't inappropriate with each other."

I catch sight of DeeDee watching our conversation from a distance.

He sets his bag at his feet. "Did you have fun at the party at Al-Hidaayah?"

"How did you know about that?" I wiggle my index finger at him. "Are you a stalker?"

"Just well connected."

"Explain please." I'm staring. His burgundy sweater and dark-washed jeans are a good look on him.

"My sister is a senior at that school."

Being the topic of some random girl's conversation isn't my favorite thing. "I had a good time. The food was amazing, and I brought a ton of candy back for both me and DeeDee."

Maybe she telepathically knew I said her name, because she joins us. "Hello," she says to Muhammad. "L, you haven't picked out a single book yet. We're not staying here all day."

My death glare doesn't affect her at all.

"Sorry, that's my fault. I've been distracting her." Mo grins. So, so hot. "It was good to see both of you again. Enjoy the sale."

I watch him walk away, then shove my bestie's shoulder. "Whyyy?"

"What?" She points at herself. "No thanks for saving your ass? He *doesn't date*, remember. So his flirting was totally unnecessary."

Is that what that was?

When my reusable bag is loaded with my five fantasy finds, I join DeeDee in the graphic novel section.

"Why did you talk to him for so long, anyway? You like him that much?" She winks at me, then heads towards the registers with some comics. Just like her to voice a truth I'm too scared to say. Rushing to catch up with her, I swerve to avoid bumping into another customer heading in the same direction. "Girl, wait for me!"

As DeeDee gets to the cashier, I push past her. "Nope, you planned this entire day. I got these."

After spending eight dollars for the ten books between us, we leave the building and climb into her car.

182

"So, what's next?"

"We haven't been to Plato's Closet in forever. You down?"

Go to my favorite consignment store, without any time constraints? "I'm in." My mind flashes back to her last challenge. "Look, Muhammad is nice to look at but I found out at the Muslim party that plenty of girls are interested and he follows the 'no dating' thing."

My bestie pulls out of the parking space and circles the block to get to I-25. "He was a topic of conversation. That's interesting."

The *I-told-you-so* in her tone irks me.

"Think your families will push the two of you together if your aunt has her way?"

"Getting married or even engaged before graduating high school is a huge HELL NO." I open the dashboard heating vents and point them in my direction. "You know me."

She shrugs her shoulders like it's not a statement of fact. "I thought I did. You going to the mosque and the Muslim girls' party are new things. I'm still getting used to them." Her voice takes a different tone. "Should I be worried?"

"About what exactly?"

We pass three mile markers before she answers.

"Well, if you do move...just theoretically...what will happen to us? The Stewarts will expect you to make new friends, Muslim ones. A new school means a new social circle, one that won't include me. Your grandfather will probably get you a car, a nice one—not like my piece of shit. The new Leena will change into someone I don't recognize and might not even like."

My best friend has never been like this before—it's a new version of her *I* don't recognize.

"DeeDee, you already know we're ride-or-die. Nothing will change that." Her honesty, her vulnerability, it hurts me. "No matter where I live, you are everything to me. You and my mom."

"When does your grandfather expect an answer?" She takes the next exit.

"Soon."

Thinking about how my life could totally change sucks. What if everything she's saying happens? I don't *want* to become a different person. I don't *want* to live up to a totally new set of unrealistic expectations.

DeeDee parks, and we step inside the consignment store. I put a fake smile on my face, picking up a few items I don't even like.

"Look at these jeans, L. I'm definitely trying them on."

I nod.

An hour later, my BFF has been in the dressing room three times and is paying for her two pairs of jeans and a cute set of earrings. Me, I'm empty-handed. We ride home, not talking, but listening to an R&B oldies radio station.

Back in my bedroom, I arrange my new-to-me books on my TBR shelf. With phone in hand, I settle on my bed and start a new note.

PROS OF MOVING:
- Attending a better school, more classes to choose from
- Getting into a top university
- Connecting with my grandfather and Samira (big maybe)
- Home-cooked meals
- Getting a car? Maybe a new phone?
- Seeing Muhammad again

CONS OF MOVING:
- Leaving my mom by herself/Her hating me
- Losing contact with DeeDee
- Starting a new school & making friends
- Being pressured to become a Muslim
- My grandfather's academic expectations

A thought more terrifying than these hits me.

My eyes scan my vast collection of books. If my aunt *ever* tried to censor what I read, I'd lose it. She can't be that extreme, can she?

A text comes in.

> Not going to be home until late. I'm tired already.

My mom is a true homebody. I answer her.

> Drink some coffee. Have fun!! 🦆

My rumbling stomach reminds me it's past dinnertime. Two minutes later, I'm at the kitchen counter, making a peanut-butter-and-honey sandwich. Adding a peeled Cutie to the plate completes my meal.

Aunt Samira's ringtone interrupts the silence. I race to answer her. "Hi!"

"Hello, Leena. I'm glad you answered. We need to talk."

My heartbeat is officially racing—this can't be good. "Okay, what's up?" I just want to hide under my comforter.

After a moment of silence, she clears her throat. "We're both serious about our offer. Are you?"

"I told my mom about it, so..."

"Good, because you can't pretend that you want a real relationship with my brother, then take lightly something he asks of you. I won't tolerate any type of disrespect in his life."

What? She's so mad, and for what? This is messing with my head. "Are you angry with me?"

"No." She exhales. "I'm trying to ensure that you don't break your grandfather's heart, like your mother did."

Unbelievable.

"So it's all Mom's fault?" I ask, already heated. "After she lost *her* mother, had her entire life turned inside out, and had a baby, you're still angry at her. How can you be? You even took away her martial arts training!"

"Is that all she told you?" The response is fast. "Did my niece mention she threw a fit simply because we insisted that one of us accompany her to tournaments? Tariq stood his ground, so instead of going with her coach to that year's state competition, she did not."

Her sharp words hit me like a slap. "You stole that from her."

"Your grandfather and I don't hold the past against you. InshaALLAH, you're a smarter young lady than she was, with a brighter future."

"Wait." Without waiting for permission, I put the call on mute.

I pace for an entire minute. "Who the hell does she think she is?" My words hang in the air. She's my aunt. And it sounds like she doesn't want me to move in.

I unmute. "If you're so against this, why did I get the invitation?"

"My brother thinks it's for the best. But there are too many issues that should've been discussed beforehand. Certain expectations needed to be set."

My fingers grip my phone tighter.

"And what are those *expectations*?"

"No smoking, drinking, or drug use. No cell phones after nine p.m. on school nights. A healthy diet. High academic achievement. We'd develop a more complete list if you move in."

My heart's pounding in my chest. "Anything else? Off the top of your head."

"For me, the main one is that you don't engage in any behaviors while living here that lead you to become a teenage mother."

Rage and deep sadness battle inside me.

She doesn't just dislike me. This woman thinks my whole life, the fact that I'm breathing, is a sin—a belief that hasn't budged since we met.

Everything about this is sick.

"I get it now. Thanks. I gotta go."

I tap the call closed, and then I crumble. Wave after wave of tears fall down my face and soak into the carpet. I wait for the pain wracking my body to disappear, but it doesn't. And it won't.

Move over, DeeDee. Disappointment is my new best friend.

CHAPTER NINETEEN

February

Opening my eyes this morning is a chore.

But the smoky aroma of grilled meat pushes me out of the bed. After a stop in the hallway bathroom to splash water on my face, my growling stomach leads me through the living room into the kitchen.

"Ma, are you feeling okay?"

She's standing at the stove, scrambling eggs. "I'm good. You?"

I grab a piece of turkey bacon off a plate in the middle of the table. "Better now." When it's gone, I claim a second one. "But you're making a legit breakfast?"

Instead of an answer, she divides the food on two paper plates. "You don't want any?"

"Not so fast. I never said that." I take one of the servings. "Just wondering if it's a special occasion or something. It smells delicious."

"No reason. I just wanted to eat something other than cereal."

"Well. Thank you! Maybe this can be our new Sunday breakfast tradition."

My mom snaps her fingers in my direction. "If you agree to help out with the cooking, *maybe*."

I want to smile...

...but a replay of every hideous thing Samira said to me last night is on repeat in my head. I sneak glances at my mom. *Should I tell her?* She seems cheerful. Probably shouldn't ruin it.

Maybe...maybe if Aunt Samira saw more of me on a regular basis (and this might take months), we could get along better. Assuming I still want to get along with her.

My mom finishes off the rest of her breakfast, then throws out her empty paper plate.

"Ma, can we talk about Tariq? Or to him? The offer...We should discuss it as a family. Right?"

Her jaw softens—pure honesty is working. "If you're serious, I'll go with you. Don't expect me to be happy about it, but someone needs to protect you from their scheming."

Suddenly, my phone lights up, a picture of my aunt filling the screen.

"Hi, Aunt Samira." I'm not interested in a repeat of yesterday's conversation. What does she want?

"Let me speak to Asiyah. *Now*." She sounds even meaner than last night.

I hold my phone out. "Ma, Samira wants to talk to you."

"Hello, why didn't you call me directly?" my mom asks, sounding as cold as I did. And then—her face drains of color.

My mouth dries up. "Ma, what's wrong?"

She refuses to look at me. Tears are running down her cheeks.

I rush to her side.

"We'll be there." Mom's lips are pressed into a thin line. "Within thirty minutes. Unless you keep me on the phone with your *stupid* questions. Bye."

"Ma?" I ask, horrified. "What...?"

She gives me back my phone. "Sit down, Leena."

I want to, but my legs aren't working.

"Your grandfather had another heart attack early this morning." She grabs my hands. "He didn't make it."

My legs collapse under me. "**NO!**"

Of course, Mom catches me, preventing a fall. "Leena, I'm so sorry. Samira isn't handling it well and demanded we meet her at the hospital. Are you up for that? If not, I can go by myself."

Shaking my head, I whisper to her, "I'll be okay. Let me throw some clothes on. I *want* to go."

We step into the waiting room. Samira is there, the devastated look on her face as somber as her plain, all-black abaya. A nurse is beside her.

"Follow me," Samira whispers.

We do.

Walking through the double doors, the staff stares at us. Not a single word is spoken. One older man, in a white doctor's coat, gives us a sad sympathy smile. My body is numb. All I can do is put one foot in front of the other.

Samira stops. Her stiff body language scares the hell out of me.

"Tariq is in there. Asiyah, you and your daughter can go in together, or one at a time. InshaALLAH, brothers from the Islamic Center are on their way to claim the body."

My mom's answer is immediate. "We'll go together."

Inside the quiet hospital room, a single bed is the only piece of furniture. My grandfather's whole body is covered with a thin white sheet. A part of me wants to turn and run, but my mom joins her hand to mine. "You don't have to do this, Leena."

I wince back tears. "No...we should each say goodbye."

After enfolding me in a tight hug, my mom lets go, walks over, and pulls back the sheet.

Tariq's eyes are closed, but if I didn't know better, I'd bet he was asleep.

Mom leans in and whispers something in her dad's ear. Then she returns to my side. "Take your time."

I silent-shuffle to his bedside. My heart is breaking into a million tiny shards. My final whispers aren't much, but they're all I have.

"I'm sorry we didn't have more time together. I loved getting to know you. Thank you for letting me into your life."

We leave.

Before either of us can say anything, Aunt Samira gets right into my mom's face in the hall. "Are you happy now? He's gone! ALLAH called him back, and there's no opportunity for the two of you to reconcile. Family is *everything*, and you threw it all away."

It's too much.

"Samira, why are you so mean? So mean and so *horrible*?" A tidal wave of anger rolls over me. "How is bringing up the past helping anyone right now?"

My aunt's face goes lobster red. "Talking to your elders in such a *disrespectable* way tells me exactly how you were raised."

Reaching for my hand, Mom snaps back. "I'm not doing this in public. We've all lost something. I know that being spiteful is your specialty, but we're not staying here to listen to it. I'm sure his granddaughter would like to attend the Janaza prayer. Text me the details when you get over yourself."

She speed-walks away from our toxic family member, with me half-running to keep up.

A heavy silence hangs between us the whole way home.

Back in the kitchen, my mom says, "Are you okay?"

"Not really."

The sadness seeping from her makes me tear up again. "If you're tired, honey, go get some sleep. The funeral could be as early as this afternoon."

"Wait...what? You're kidding, right?"

"No, I'm not. If possible, Muslims try to bury their dead within twenty-four hours after a person's death. Three days is usually the max."

I use my last few drops of energy to keep my face blank. "Promise you'll wake me up if you hear from Samira."

She springs out of her chair and hugs me. "I promise."

Once I'm behind my closed bedroom door, I reread Tariq's last email to me.

Miss you, Grandfather.
I love you.

That reply will live forever in my drafts folder.

Curling up in the fetal position with a blanket over me, I hug my star pillow and close my eyes until sleep welcomes me.

≈

"Leena, Leena?" My mom's voice stirs me awake. "Time to get ready. Deidre should be here soon."

Pushing myself up, I ask, "Why?"

"I called her," she admits. "Don't you want your best friend with you at the masjid?"

The best parent award—hers.

Thirty minutes later, I'm clean and dressed in the loosest pair of pants in my closet. I step into the living room and catch sight of DeeDee.

She rushes over to me and hesitates only a nanosecond before throwing her arms around me. "How are you doing?"

My girl isn't really touchy-feely, so I'm extra grateful for the hug. "Not sure." I squeeze her back. "Thanks for being here."

"Let's go, girls. Samira will notice if we're even a minute late."

After grabbing our coats, the three of us pile into my mom's car.

As we pull into the masjid's parking lot, DeeDee grips my hand. Once we're all out of the sedan, she and I follow behind Mom through the door labeled WOMEN'S AREA.

"Shoes go there." My mom points to the tall bookcase.

The light cream walls and flowery throw pillows are fighting with the massive black leather furniture. A row of folding chairs stretches across the back wall. Two ladies wearing decorated black abayas stop their conversation and look our way.

Hope we're all dressed okay. My BFF's all-black clothes and my mom's navy-blue skirt and blouse look fine to me. But I'm not Muslim, so what do I know?

My sock-covered feet make no sound as we enter a prayer space, exactly like the men's where the Imam talked to us at the youth event. Dozens of Muslim women are already here.

"Stay close, girls." My mom doesn't have to repeat herself.

Seconds later, Rheem is walking towards me. Instead of black, she's wearing an ankle-length burgundy dress with a cream headscarf.

The perfect time for a friendly face.

"Leena." She wraps me into a quick hug. "I'm glad you came. Brother Tariq was loved in this community." Rheem points to the large group of men on the other side of the one-way glass. "A lot of people are here to pray for him. That's a good thing in our faith. If you have questions about what's going on, please just ask."

"Hey, thanks." I don't have words right now. "This is my best friend, DeeDee."

They exchange sad smiles.

A door on the far wall opens. Samira walks out, making a beeline to us.

My Muslim friend sees her too. "In a few weeks, you, me, and DeeDee should get brunch—if you're up to it. I really mean it. Text me."

She rushes away just in time.

"Better late than never, Asiyah. At least the Janaza hasn't started yet." Samira's gaze rolls over Mom. "Just for your father's funeral, you couldn't cover your hair? Is nothing sacred to you anymore?"

My mouth drops open.

"Yelling at me and my daughter at the hospital was bad enough, but here, in the musallah? And you're questioning *me* about sacred spaces?"

Mom's accusation scores a direct hit. My aunt has no comeback.

The imam's wife slides up beside us. "Sister Samira, there are a few women from the interfaith community in the multipurpose room. They're asking for you."

Aunt Samira walks away without saying another word.

"Hello, Leena. I'm so sorry for your loss. Brother Tariq was very knowledgeable and kindhearted. He will be missed."

"Thank you," I say. "Mom, this is Maryam, the Imam's wife." My bestie nudges me with her elbow. "And you remember Deidre."

Sister Maryam nods. "Of course, I remember both of you." Turning to my mother, she says, "If there's anything you need, please, please let me know. The Imam and I are here for the entire Stewart family. Your father was a great man."

The three of us each sit in the back of the prayer space, in the first row of chairs. My eyes are glued to my mom.

My greatest wish, to be one big, happy extended family, is gone.

"Leena, are you doing okay? We can leave if you're uncomfortable," my mom whispers.

"Not sure *what* I'm feeling. But it seems wrong to miss this."

Mom squeezes my shoulder. "Okay. The funeral prayer doesn't last that long anyway."

Before I can ask her to explain, the sisters line up shoulder to shoulder. My great-aunt is among them. A male voice from the loudspeaker recites a phrase over and over again. Each time, those praying raise their hands to their ears, then cross them over their chest. One, two, three, four times as the loudspeaker guy recites something in a language I don't recognize. Then women turn their heads to the right. Then, some head towards the door while others surround Samira.

"Ma, is that it?" A couple of minutes is all my grandfather gets?

She nods. "Most of the men and a few ladies will accompany the body to the cemetery and stay until after the burial."

All these new facts are swimming around in my head—not knowing where to land.

"Does Samira just...go home by herself?" DeeDee asks tentatively.

My mom shakes her head. "I bet a ton of women will be there with her, and each of them will bring food. They'll make sure your great-aunt isn't alone." She glances around the room. "Leena, do you want to go to the cemetery?"

A super simple question. And a super simple answer. "NO."

"You don't need to yell; we're both here beside you." I swear I can hear the relief in DeeDee's voice.

"Let's go." My mom gets no argument from me.

The three of us head back to the car.

"You think Aunt Samira will be mad we left without saying goodbye?"

"To be honest...I don't care."

Mom turns on her favorite oldies station and tunes everything else out as she drives us home. Out of the corner of my eye, I watch my best friend instead. Talking about death is something she hates doing—if *I* lost both my parents and had to live with a relative who reminded me constantly how much my presence was a burden, *I'd* never bring up the subject either.

The thin hold on my emotions breaks.

Tears course down my cheeks. I turn towards the window. Then there are fingers on my shoulder. Without turning around, I put my hand over DeeDee's.

CHAPTER TWENTY

March

Life goes back to its regular routine.

Except no one talks about the Stewart only sixty miles north of us.

Or the one we just lost.

Going to school, then work, sometimes six days a week, is my new normal. Except her occasional date with Quan, my bestie and I are almost always together in our free time. We can't get enough of the discount movie theater, the library (that's more me), or our favorite burger spot in town. It keeps my heart from getting too heavy, and it helps her stay out of Lilian's way.

Finally, spring break arrives on a Friday afternoon.

At Asiyah's Angels, we've scrubbed down every surface. That's after we picked up every block, straightened up the crayon corner, and cleared the couch cushions of every gummy bear stashed underneath.

"You two have any plans tonight?" My mom's sitting at the table, a tall glass of water in front of her.

"We could get some Blake's for dinner."

"L, you're addicted to them or something. Isn't there a support group for that?"

"What do *you* want to eat?" I sniff. "And don't say sushi."

A knock at the door forces me to sit up.

"Did one of you order something without telling me?" Mom heads to the door.

"Nope—not me." DeeDee points at me. "Although you look hella guilty." I roll my eyes.

But a delivery person isn't there.

It's my aunt.

The aunt we haven't seen or communicated with since Tariq's funeral five weeks ago.

"Salaam, Asiyah." Her voice is unemotional. "We need to talk, all three of us. Can I come in?"

My mom's hands ball up into fists, then relax. She opens her mouth, but instead of answering the question, she turns to me. "Do you want to hear what Samira has to say?"

After searching my aunt's face, I nod. "Yes."

The hem of my great-aunt's dark grey abaya sweeps over the doorframe as she enters.

DeeDee scrambles off the couch. "I think that's my cue." She sprints out the door, closing it behind her.

Mom gestures to the modest kitchen. "We can talk here."

Three generations of Stewart women around the same table. *Our* table. Never thought this would happen.

"Tariq's lawyer contacted me yesterday. He left something for each of you in his will." Samira rests her clenched hands on the table, her jaw just as tight.

Mom's eyes widen. "He did?"

No small talk; we're jumping right into it.

She nods. "Of course. That's what kind of man he was. MashaALLAH, kind and generous. You don't have anything more to say, Asiyah?"

The woman who raised me, alone, without a penny from her family takes a long sip of her water. "It really kills you that he did that, doesn't it? What, you think there's not enough to go around?"

Samira blows out an angry breath.

"Why would you want anything from him now? You abandoned him. It broke his heart. His only child—gone."

She either really loved her brother or really hates her niece.

Mom's hand slaps the tabletop, *hard*. Her glass even shakes. "Don't forget how much of a part YOU played in me running away. Super judgmental person you have always been. Not much has changed." She points at me. "But now there's two of us. Anything that helps me, helps Leena as well. Why would you be salty about that?"

"My grandfather didn't want this," I say, although I don't know where the words come from. "Family might not be important to either of you, but it is to me." I swivel towards

Samira. "Just because you're fine being alone, ignoring the only remaining Stewarts in the world, doesn't mean I am." I swivel towards Mom. "Ma, I need you to be a hundred percent in my corner, even when I do stuff you don't agree with. I want to stay connected to my grandfather's legacy. Can we do that?"

They're both looking down, avoiding eye contact with anyone.

Before losing my new confidence, I blurt out, "What do we need to do now? To find out about his will?"

My aunt straightens her back. "The three of us need to meet with his lawyer, who is also the executor." She gets up. "Leena, please text me your final decision."

I walk her to the front door. "I will. Thanks for coming over and telling us in person." Maybe it's better for everyone Samira isn't staying a minute longer.

Once she leaves, I rejoin my mom at the table.

"You hungry? We need to decide on dinner."

"Ma, please, let's talk about what just happened. We both need to be less avoidant."

She actually shakes her head. "Nope. Food first."

I press my hands to my hips. "Fine, let's have pizza."

It takes at least sixty seconds—I'm counting—for her to place the order on the phone. "Okay, done. Are you happy now?"

"Are you ever going to stop hating Samira? I don't. Maybe she thought you'd find comfort in your faith to help get over your mom's death. Like Tariq did. Have you ever asked Samira what it was like to lose her husband?"

She rises, closes the blinds, and comes back. "I don't *hate* her."

"Sounds like that to me," I tell her while digging into the bag of pita chips that lives on the kitchen table.

"It's complicated."

My loud crunching is the only sound in the room.

"You already know the whole sordid story. After my mom died, I just wanted to feel normal again. But my aunt moved in with us, to *help*, and all she brought with her were impossible standards and harshness. Your grandfather let her in, and didn't do a *damn* thing about his sister's cruelty."

Her words bruise my heart.

"I needed someone to talk to but neither of them would listen."

And now I ask the hardest question. "Is that why you're not a Muslim anymore?"

"Organized religions aren't my thing." Her face drops. "I couldn't take it anymore. My whole life changed. No more martial arts, no more public school, only what she thought was 'appropriate.' It was like I lost both parents that year."

Scooting my chair closer to hers, I grab her hand.

"Your dad and I were just martial arts buddies. When tae kwon do was taken away, we ended up just texting friends…and then my home situation erupted. He was so supportive, such a good listening ear. As a Black girl in the Islamic school, being one of the two African American faces, my friend circle was already small. I needed that friendship. But when my aunt found out I was still in touch with Mateo, things got much worse in the house."

It's like she's describing a Netflix special, not her own life. "How?"

"I told you. They had a plan. I overheard Samira and my dad arranging a dinner with some brother, someone who was coming over the next night to meet me. They said it would be a great match for both of us, and maybe if I was married, I'd settle down."

"Wait...how old were you?" My math isn't mathing.

"The same age you are right now." She looks past me. "The next day, instead of my homework and textbooks, I stuffed my backpack with clothes. Mateo was down the street from the school, waiting for me. I left my entire life behind." Mom grips my hand. "Does that answer your question about me and the faith community I was raised in?"

After that outpouring, asking anything else is impossible.

A new notification comes in.

> L, you want to come over? Lilian okayed it. Can be there in twenty. You still stuck in the family drama?

> Let me ask.

Glancing over my shoulder, I ask, "Are we finished talking? DeeDee wants me to spend the night."

My mom says, "That's fine—we probably both need some time."

After a quick change of clothes, I pull my thick curly hair into a quick ponytail and stash an extra outfit in a small duffle. With the addition of my pj's and a Ziploc bag of my essential bathroom things, I'm set.

I step into my Converse. "Ma, you going to be okay by yourself?"

"Go, have fun. Just don't make a mess over there. Lilian's no joke."

≈

"Is your grandmother really okay with me sleeping over? Last time, she complained we were too loud and dirtied up her kitchen."

"She's on her way to a new bingo game. Problem solved. Maybe she'll win big and be in a good mood the next time we see her."

I cross my fingers. "Let's hope."

We each slip out of our shoes—can't forget. Avoiding Lilian's wrath is essential. I turn left and, halfway down the hall, head through DeeDee's bedroom door.

"Hold up. Let me put the towel down." My bestie spreads a stained old towel across her full-size mattress.

"Thanks." After setting down our pizza, I scramble to the right side of the bed (AKA my side).

"So, what happened after I left?"

Not one with a ton of patience; I'm not surprised by her directness. "Let me eat a slice before the interrogation. Damn." On purpose, I take extra time to chew each bite.

"Girl, stop." She pushes my shoulder. "It's going to take you half an hour to get to your crust."

I wipe the corners of my mouth. "My aunt told us that my grandfather left us something in his will."

DeeDee swivels in my direction. "So, you've got an inheritance now. Wow! Soon, you really *will* be too good to hang out with my broke ass."

"HA HA. You're not funny." I crumple up a napkin and launch it at her. "You can't get rid of me that easy—or ever. This is a life-sentence kind of relationship. Anyway, until we meet with the lawyer, I won't have any details. It could be fifty bucks."

She frowns. "What about your mom? Does she have an issue with getting something from Tariq? Or with *you* getting something, specifically?"

DeeDee is super smart.

"Nope. When my aunt brought up some nonsense about that, Mom shut her down." The sides of my mouth arc upwards.

"Oooh, this is juicy. Samira must be pissed."

That's an understatement.

"If you accept whatever is in his will, do you think your aunt will ever speak to you again?"

Her question is like an unexpected punch to the gut. Feels like my family's gone before I ever knew them.

"Have no idea." All talked out, I grab another slice.

She switches on the TV. "Fine. Let's watch something." She scoots away from me. "It's my turn to choose, and we *won't* be watching fantasy—deal with it. I'm in the mood for car chases and wildly over-the-top fight scenes."

I fold my bottom lip down into a pout. She grins, not affected in the least.

Here, in her room, my stress melts away. No judgment, no expectations, just a soft place to land.

≈

"L, get up."

I rub my eyes, DeeDee's face way too close to mine. "What time is it?"

She points to the bright sunlight streaming through her only window. "I heard movement upstairs. Lilian is probably already awake but last night's trash is still in the kitchen."

Shit.

We work as a team.

My bestie leads the way.

She shoves everything from last night's meal in a trash bag and heads out the front door while I use a disinfecting wipe to clean the counter. After inspecting the tile under my feet, I grab the broom from the hall closet and sweep the kitchen floor.

By the time her grandmother wanders into the kitchen, we're each done with our two-pack of Pop-Tarts. "Good morning, Leena. How are you?"

The flowing ankle-length caftan and kitten-heel slippers are her usual morning finery, but the tight bun on top of her head is immaculate—not a hair out of place.

"I'm okay, Lilian. Thanks for asking."

Out of the corner of my eye, I catch DeeDee staring into her half-empty glass of tap water.

"According to your friend here, your long-lost extended family is Muslim. Be careful—you're already Black and a woman. If you convert, that'll be your third strike."

I feel my eyes widen.

"Lilian, that's screwed up. Why would you say that?" My BFF voices her opinion.

I kick her leg under the table. It's way too early for a confrontation.

Her grandmother's blank expression is still strong. As soon as her electric kettle whistles, she pours some hot water, adds her Lipton tea bag and five sugars to her mug, then joins us at their kitchen table. "It's the truth. Being an adult isn't fun and games. No one owes you anything—don't see the point of making life harder for yourself."

DeeDee's hand is clenched. "Self-hate doesn't help anyone."

Lilian's jaw steels. Daggers of anger are hitting her only grandchild. "That's not what I said, Deidre." She leans back in her chair. "I love what I see in the mirror every day but you young people today need a dose of reality. Life throws tests at everyone all the time."

"Aren't you tired from always being so negative?" My BFF is riled up.

But her only living family member isn't having it.

"I'm not negative—I'm real. What pisses me off is this back-and-forth." She's points at both of us. "Accepting wisdom from someone who's been alive almost a half a century more than you is a lesson you haven't learned yet. You'd think how I took you in after your parents were killed would be enough to show you that life's not fair."

It's a super low blow. Time's up.

"DeeDee, I need to get home soon," I say. "It was nice to see you, Lilian."

"Bye."

Thirty minutes later, we're both clean, dressed, and rushing out of this negative space.

"Sorry for that, L. I thought she'd be nicer." These are the first two complete sentences my BFF has said to me since the kitchen table argument. "A hundred percent wrong on that."

I look up from my phone. "Don't worry—I'm used to Lilian. That's what I don't want in a relationship with Samira."

As we stop at a red light, she glances at me. "What are you going to do? Cut her off since you said her and your mom are toxic together?"

DeeDee pulls into my driveway before I know how to answer that.

"My grandfather was thoughtful enough to name me in his will, so I'm going to meet with the lawyer." Saying the words out loud to another person strengthens me. "My aunt and my mom need to grow up and at least be polite to each other."

"Listen to you, Miss Confident. You tell 'em."

I'm talking a good game, but I have no idea what will happen the next time the three Stewart women end up in the same room.

Guess we'll find out.

CHAPTER TWENTY-ONE

March

I ease the door shut, not wanting to make a ton of noise before 9 a.m. on a Saturday.

"Good morning. Didn't think you'd be home so early."

My heart jumps into my throat.

Waist-deep in paperwork, my mom's taken over half the kitchen table. "Get yourself some breakfast—we both know Lilian cooks less than I do."

Instead, I snag a juice box.

Sitting across from her, doubts creep into my brain. Maybe I should make a pro and con list about this inheritance.

"So, tell me. How are you feeling about the will? What about Samira? You okay with seeing her again?"

The baby hairs on the back of my neck stand up.

No avoiding the hard stuff this morning.

After a sip of my super sweet drink, I say, "Tariq left me something for a reason. I never asked him for anything—the new laptop was a complete surprise. She might disagree but it's the truth."

"One thing I can say, your great-aunt hasn't changed much since I was your age. She's exactly the same." My mom shrugs. "A consistent bitch is a real one."

"Ma!" She hates it when I use that kind of language.

After gulping down the rest of her coffee, she winks at me. "Sorry but I had to live with her—that means I can admit the ugly truth."

Hatred is flowing from her entire body, even her pores.

I gulp down my growing dread. "If I wanted you to, would you go with me?"

Staring right into my soul, her gaze doesn't waver. "Is that what you really want?"

"I think so," I say. "But... I'm not sure you can handle it."

She scans the piles of paperwork in front of her long enough for me to think she forgot I'm here.

"If you're sure, like a hundred percent, you're okay with sitting in a room with HER, hearing what your grandfather left you, and dealing with the aftermath of it all—then I have to go."

I scramble out of my chair and wrap my arms around her shoulders. "Going by myself would've been messed up."

She pats my arms. "Remember you said that when Samira and I end up in a screaming match in the estate lawyer's office." My mom leaves her dirty cup in the sink.

I'm back in my chair when my stomach wakes up.

"Do we have any of my favorite cereal left?"

"Nope." She pulls the yellow box off the top of the fridge. "If you're going to be one of those wealthy Stewarts, no more sugary cereal. Here you go."

"Ha ha. A career in stand-up isn't in your future." Just to show her, I get a bowl and fill it up for myself. Drowning it in milk and three spoonfuls of sugar helps me get it down.

It takes me a minute but I look over at my mom.

"Go ahead, laugh." I tap my finger in the table space between us. "My sweet tooth is completely your fault. You gave me too many Dum-Dums when I was a kid."

"Guilty as charged. You should be thanking me. A childhood with good memories can't be replaced. It should be treasured." Without warning or a single word, she gets up, squeezes my shoulder, then walks down the hall. As soon as her bedroom door closes, a little louder than usual, I get it.

I force down the rest of my now-soggy cereal. My foot keeps tapping the carpet under the table. Maybe us going through with this isn't the smartest thing to do—rehashing old pain isn't my intention.

But it might be unavoidable.

The Stewart family is a hot mess.

≈

Nothing in the past few days prepares me for this heaviness in my stomach as we sit unnaturally straight in the waiting room. My mom's sporting a pair of business suit pants and a blouse. I'm wearing a knee-length skirt and off-white polo shirt. Everything is last-minute finds from Goodwill.

Not like I'm wearing either of them again.

My legs won't stay still. From crossing them at the ankles stretched out in front of me to keeping my feet and knees together, I can't get comfortable. "Ma, do you think she's coming?"

"Samira definitely won't miss today—I'm sure nothing but getting hit by a truck would keep her away."

"That's terrible! Don't even joke like that." I rub my hands down my lap. "Maybe there's a ton of traffic on I25."

"She's lived in Santa Fe forever—she knows how much time it takes to get here. It's not Balloon Fiesta time of year; it's a regular Wednesday morning." Mom's frown might be permanent. "Having to tell my families I couldn't watch their kids today wasn't any fun. Losing out on money makes me cranky."

"At least everyone understood. At least that's what they said in the cards they sent us. I left them on the kitchen table. You probably didn't even read any of them."

She shrugs and goes back to the Wordle game on her phone.

I try to read a book on my Kindle app but my concentration is close to zero. Instead, I stare at the elevator doors.

After I count to two hundred in my head, my aunt steps out of the elevator.

"She's here," I whisper in my mom's ear.

Immediately, Mom's eyes narrow while she tucks her Samsung Galaxy into her purse.

"Hello, Leena, Asiyah." Samira's all-black abaya and headscarf make a statement but the smile on her face looks genuine.

"Hi," I answer back.

All my mom manages to say is, "Hey."

It's our good luck (I guess we'll see) that a tall man in a navy-blue suit approaches us. "Salaam, Sister Samira. Thank you for coming." He turns towards us. "This must be Asiyah and Leena. Nice to meet both of you."

We stand.

"Hello. Yes, that's us." Mom's normal tone is gone, replaced with one flat as a tortilla without a drop of emotion.

Can't blame her—we both expect this to hurt more than period cramps.

"Hello, I'm Mr. Pierce, Tariq's attorney." He keeps his hands at his sides. "Please, everyone, follow me."

He leads us into a large conference room; the dark wood table is surrounded by oversized chairs. The faint scent of Pledge hits my nostrils. Samira is across from us while the lawyer claims the seat in front of a big manila folder. "If you'd like something to drink, please let me know. We have coffee, tea, and bottled water. My assistant can bring in whatever you like."

"It's best we get started."

Samira's order shouldn't surprise me but it does.

Mr. Pierce nods. "Okay." He opens the file in front of him, then picks up the first page. "First, let me say, I'm sorry for your family's loss. Tariq was my client for more than a decade—I considered him a friend."

"Thank you, Mustafa." My aunt seems to know this man. "My brother was very fond of you too."

Mom is bouncing her knee under the table.

"So, Brother Tariq designated me as the executor of his estate. I reread the document last week, and he was adamant that everything be done according to Islam as much as possible."

Clearing her throat, my mom asks, "Did he put any conditions on any of the inheritances?"

Why would she even think something like that?

The lawyer doesn't flinch. "No, not a one."

I feel a smile building on my face. "My grandfather was a good man."

I scan the room; finally something most of us agree with.

"Tariq bequeathed everything in his estate to be left to three of you," he continues. "In different percentages."

My aunt is perched on the edge of her chair. "Meaning?"

Mr. Pierce faces her. "Miss Stewart, your brother made sure you had an equal share in both the house and the businesses. We're all here so I can let you all know how he wanted his fifty percent of both of those distributed."

Wait...what?

"I'm only sixteen. How can I be part owner of a huge house in Santa Fe?" Maybe it's a cruel joke, but after checking this guy's face, I know this is absolutely real.

Across the table, Samira's face is now crimson. "I suppose this means moving is in my future—from somewhere I've lived for almost twenty years. Astaghfirullah."

"Aunt Samira, me or my mom aren't going to throw you out of your house." My gentle words don't move the scowl on her face. "Right, Ma?"

She smirks before saying, "I'm not interested in moving to Santa Fe or selling the house there. No reason for anyone to move."

An older lady, in a light beige pantsuit and plain black heels, comes into the room. She sets down an assortment of drinks. There are also mini pastries, biscuits, and small cups of donut holes. She walks to each of us, extending the tray. When we each have something, she says, "I'll just leave the rest here. Please help yourselves."

"Thank you, Miss Garcia."

Once she's gone, Mom downs half a mini water bottle. "What exactly does any of this mean, Mr. Pierce?"

"Your father was an intelligent man. He worked hard in corporate America for decades and opened several small businesses after retirement." The lawyer reaches over, snagging one of the small cups of donut holes. He pops one in his mouth. When it's gone, he says, "Sorry, I didn't eat anything this morning."

My mom actually cracks a smile. "Doesn't bother me—no worries."

Samira, across the room, folds her arms across her chest. She doesn't even try to hide her frown.

Mr. Pierce shuffles the papers in front of him, then pulls out a thick document. "In simplified terms, Asiyah, you're entitled to twenty-five percent of all your dad's fifty percent share of the assets. Then, Leena's share and Samira's shares are about eight and seventeen percent, respectively."

My head hurts.

"Per this document, Asiyah will inherit half of what was Tariq's share of all his business interests. Same for the house and any liquid assets."

The conference room is so quiet, we can all hear a police siren outside—a normal thing in downtown Albuquerque. "Do we have to accept whatever he left us?"

The words pop out of my mouth.

"That's a great question, Leena." He scans the table, then refocuses on me. "Of course you don't. Brother Tariq was very intentional in making sure the three of you were provided for. Since this estate is worth between three to four million dollars, please take some time to think about everything if that's what you need to do."

My throat is now super dry.

I reach for my fancy bottled water named after an island and take a few small sips. When I look over at my mom, she's staring straight ahead at the wall behind Samira's head.

"Ladies, please excuse me. I'll be right back." Just like that, the three Stewart women are alone.

"Did you know how much money he had?" Mom is focused, her accusation for her aunt.

She turns towards me, a hard look in her eyes—but there's a sadness there too. "Not really. We didn't discuss money... but I was aware he paid the house off several years ago. My brother oversaw all our financial matters. It was one of his strengths."

"Ma," I venture, "what happens now?"

Without being asked, Samira answers. "Well, I'll have to wait for your decisions. Then *another* meeting with Mr. Pierce will be mandatory." She glares in our direction. "We'll also have to discuss what should happen with the businesses. But I can't imagine either of you will have strong opinions, since it's so unfamiliar to you."

Damn. She is definitely pissed.

Mom smirks, unfazed.

"I know nothing about business, so don't worry about me." Throwing my great-aunt a bone is all I can do.

Samira locks her gaze on my mother. "Asiyah, be honest. Any demands? Expectations?"

Mom matches her aunt's glare with one of her own. "This is so crazy, so unexpected that I need time to process it all. But you'll be the first to know."

Mr. Pierce rejoins us.

"Sorry for the delay. Leena, your grandfather wanted to make sure you earned a bachelor's degree, so he bequeathed you two hundred thousand dollars to use specifically to fulfill that goal."

All three of us Stewart women are shocked silent.

Two hundred thousand dollars! Almost a quarter of a million!

"The decedent also left each of you a monetary inheritance, according to the percentages I mentioned earlier." He takes several sips of water. "Are there any questions?"

"Yes. What exactly am I *currently* allowed to do with the businesses my brother and I owned jointly?" Samira points right at my mom. "Do I now have to include *her* in all decisions?"

Mom's face twists in a snarl, and I squeeze her hand. "Ma, please don't get loud."

"Samira, your brother gave you controlling interest in each of the businesses." Mr. Pierce hands her some papers. "If you ever sell those enterprises, then your niece must receive an appropriate portion of the proceeds." Mr. Pierce flashes us a concerned look. "Sister Samira, I think it's best for everyone concerned if you take some time to consider what's been discussed today. In fact, each of you need to make a few decisions. Then we can proceed with the next steps."

My mom and I both take the hint. She gets up first, with me seconds later.

After a loud sigh, Samira rises from her chair. "Mr. Pierce, inshaALLAH, I will contact you soon to move things forward." With those emotionless words, she strides out the door.

"Ladies, if I could offer some friendly advice," Mr. Pierce says, a gentle edge to his voice, "give Tariq's sister some time and understanding. It's an emotional time for your family—her especially."

His kindness brings a warmth inside my chest.

"Thank you for that." Mom shakes his hand.

Mr. Pierce extends a hand to me next, and I grasp it. "It was very nice to meet you both. You know, your grandfather told me about meeting you, Leena. He was impressed. And he loved spending time with you."

My throat tightens. "Thanks."

≈

I drop my grease-soaked take-out bag on the kitchen table. "Why couldn't we stay there and eat?"

Mom shakes her head. "Talking about a large inheritance in public, when you don't know who's listening—not a smart move."

Paranoid much?

"Here you go." My mom passes me two packets of malt vinegar. "Glad to see you smile. Let's talk about today. How are you feeling about all this inheritance stuff?"

I shrug.

"Come on, Leena. Not one question? You can do better than that."

My palm is itchy. Rubbing it against my thigh kinda helps. "Are we rich now?"

Instead of answering, Mom lingers over her French fries for a minute. "Well...Unless it's enough money for me to close Asiyah's Angels and move us to Hawaii, then no, I think *rich* isn't the right word to describe our new financial situation. We might be on the road to being comfortable."

"But didn't you hear I have two hundred thousand dollars for college? That's a big deal, right?"

Now she smiles. "That's a huge deal—a very generous gesture." Moving her chair closer to mine, she narrows her eyes and asks, "But do you even *want* to get a bachelor's degree after graduating high school?"

I scan the room before answering, even though I know we're alone. "Probably. Choosing what I want to study is the real problem."

"With this new college fund, money won't be something you have to worry about, at least. Most college students aren't that lucky—not the ones coming from single-parent households, anyway."

"DeeDee told me UNM is good," I offer. "She's already decided to apply there."

Mom's eyebrows crinkle. "You know I love Deidre, but please don't settle on a college based on where your best friend wants to go. It's almost as bad as basing your decision on a guy."

"Ewww. I'm not even dating anyone."

"That could change in an instant." Mom nudges me with her elbow. The late morning sun sneaks in through the vertical blinds. "Then you'll want to spend every second with the young man."

"*Ma...* Be serious. If we accept the inheritance from Tariq's will, does that mean we have to have a relationship with Samira?"

"Do you want one with her?" Mom asks.

Tough question. I count to a hundred in my head before replying.

"Leena, you've become quite a truthteller—don't stop now."

Urged on by her words, I swallow down my fear. "Yes, I do." Then I hesitate. "Could you take anything from Tariq, given your history?"

The microwave clock shows five minutes of my life have passed. Funny. I didn't realize the silence had lasted so long.

"Such a good question deserves an answer—something real." Mom catches my gaze, holding on to it. "It would be so easy to take the money and only deal with my aunt when absolutely necessary...but that feels really wrong."

"So, the answer is...?"

"I can't answer today. To be honest, right now I have no idea. My emotions are all over the place."

Maybe money *is* the root of all evil.

CHAPTER TWENTY-TWO

March

By Thursday afternoon, my mom's silence on the inheritance issue irks me more and more. It's been only twenty-four hours after meeting with the lawyer, true, but how hard can it be to accept *a ton of money?*

I know I shouldn't think that way. But it's hard.

The daycare is closed, my bed is made, a load of dark colors is in the washing machine, and I *need* to talk about this.

"Ma, what are you doing in there?"

She emerges from her room. "What, child? A grown woman can't have a minute of peace after wiping noses all week?" She's wearing a black sweater with gold buttons on the cuff and matching pants.

She looks too good to be staying home. "Where are you going?"

"If you must know, I need to get some gas—then, since our fridge is almost empty, go on a grocery store run." After grabbing her keys and purse, Mom adds, "You can come too."

I shake my head. "No thanks. DeeDee's coming back. She has major plans to get rid of her braids—it's a big hairstyle change. We need to discuss."

"Of course. I'll pick up something for dinner—for the three of us."

She leaves, and I search for sustenance. Damn, my mom is right; we don't have much food. Digging through the snack cabinet, I find half a bag of plantain chips. Bored already, I grab a fantasy book off my bookshelf and settle into the couch, wrapped in a blanket. After finishing the last page, I check my phone.

> Hey. Where r u?

An hour flies by when I'm reading.
DeeDee texts back right away.

> Sorry. Lilian got a bug up her ass about my cleaning. Just redid both bathrooms. Be there soon 🤏.

Her grandmother is super extra. I can't wait until DeeDee escapes.

My stomach growls. I'm craving nachos.

I text my mom,

> Can you get some diced jalapeños?

She knows spicy peppers are their own food group to me. I microwave a plain tortilla, then slather peanut butter all over it. Next, I search IG for nacho pictures.

By the time I'm done, she hasn't responded.

> Ma, you still at Smith's?

Maybe she's already checking out.

I open our family tracking app and check her location. She's at the gas station right beside the grocery store. Ten minutes later, her phone is still in the same place. Rising panic invades my brain.

Why isn't she answering me?

This time, texting isn't enough. I call her number.

"Hi, Leena." Her voice is almost a whisper. "Sorry I didn't answer your texts. I'm at the gas station. The police are here.... Don't worry, everything is fine now. After I give my witness statement, I'll be home."

My normal breathing hitches. "What happened?"

I count each of my breaths until she tells me.

"So a guy tried to rob the Phillips 66. I was one of the customers..." She stops talking mid-sentence. "I have to go. Please don't worry. I love you and should be home soon."

My heart's racing. Sitting down isn't an option, so moving from the living room window to my room and back again is my only way to handle what I just heard.

Every two minutes, I'm refreshing the app to see if my mom is headed back here.

Nervous tears stream down my face.

Ding. Dong.

I peek through the peephole and yank open the front door.

"Whoa. What's wrong?" DeeDee walks in.

Safely behind the closed door, I wipe my cheeks. "My mom was at the gas station by the Smith's on Tramway when someone tried to rob it!"

"Sit. Breathe."

I do and rub my eyes dry.

"Is she okay?"

"I think so...but you know her! She probably doesn't want me to freak out." Losing my mother is something I've *never* thought about. "She's all I've ever had. I love her so much."

DeeDee jumps to her feet. "What should we do? Should we go to her? It's only like ten minutes from here."

I shake my head. "APD probably won't let us get near the place."

She checks her phone. "It's over there by that expensive Glenwood Hills neighborhood. I bet the police got there super fast."

Of course, that's a thousand percent true—if it had happened anywhere on Central Avenue or in the International District, the cops would've taken forever to arrive. It's fucked up, but tonight I'm glad: My mom's safety is priority number one.

I'm pacing again.

It takes exactly twenty-four steps to get across the living room. I count them over and over. My feet are on autopilot.

The sound of a key in the lock releases me. "Mama!"

She comes through the door, three plastic grocery bags in one hand. "Hey, you two."

The nanosecond those bags land on the table, I rush her and I wrap my arms around her.

She squeezes me back. We just stay there, entangled in each other.

"Okay, Leena, I can't breathe."

I drop my arms, and we both sit. "Are you really okay?"

"Do you need anything, Asiyah?" DeeDee's enormous eyes tell me she's worried too.

Mom half-smiles. "It was really scary. But, honestly, girls, I'm just thankful no one was shot."

DeeDee gasps. "The guy had a gun?"

It would've been much better if I didn't know that particular fact.

"Yes, Deidre, he did. But the clerk kept talking to the man, as a distraction. He must have hit a silent alarm, because the APD got there in about five minutes, and he didn't have the chance to threaten me or any of the other customers."

Tears pool at the bottom of my eyes again.

Mom puts her arm around my shoulders. "I'm fine, promise. After a quick shower, everything will be almost back to normal."

She leaves the room before I can complain.

With nothing better to do, I grab the bags and transfer everything onto the kitchen counter. DeeDee joins me. I pick up the frozen veggie lasagna. She preheats the oven to four hundred degrees. "It isn't much, but we can at least get dinner started."

I nod.

By eight o'clock, we've filled our bellies, thrown away the paper plates, and put away the leftovers.

"L, I'm out." She turns to my mom and says, "Glad you didn't get hurt. You Stewarts have been through it this year."

"Thanks for staying." I nod. "Text you tomorrow."

She winks, then heads out the front door.

Then the reality of what DeeDee said hits me.

"Ma, you could've been shot and DIED."

We're both on the couch. She shifts closer to my cushion. "Leena, it's okay. I'm really fine." She holds out both her arms. "Not a scratch on me."

I glance over but still my pulse is racing like I'm watching a Jordan Peele movie in 3D. "I don't...I can't...we have to find a way to connect with Samira. If something happens to you, I'll be all alone."

She runs a hand down each of my arms. "Please don't worry. Nothing major is happening tonight. Huge decisions shouldn't be rushed."

I squirm away from her and off the couch. "Just because you ignore a situation or pretend people don't exist, doesn't mean they aren't real." I don't know if screaming or crying will help me, so I disappear into my bedroom. With the door closed, I grab the closest journal and a gel pen, before crawling onto my bed.

I find an empty page.

> A quick glimpse of normal isn't enough.
> At nine, Santa promised to bring me a family.
> In an instant, it was given, then taken away.
> Don't I deserve more than one person who gives a damn?
> Families are complicated.
> But this, it's simple.
> What's more important, working through the drama and staying together?
> Or letting the hard stuff chase you away?
> Decisions have consequences.
> The past isn't my fault.
> But I'm the one suffering.

≈

Today's six-and-a-half-hour daycare shift didn't help the nagging family thoughts inside my brain.

Being home alone, I know the next move is mine and it might go very bad. Like my-mom-may-never-forgive-me bad.

It's now or else, probably never.

After taking my phone out of my pocket, I type in a number from memory.

"Salaam, Leena."

"Hi, Samira."

"How are you?"

Without telling her the whole truth, I say, "Okay. It's been hard. We didn't have a lot of time together." I gather up a few crumbs of courage. "Do you think we could get together soon, just to talk?"

The ten-second silence between us steals my breath.

"Well, I went to Jumaah prayer today in Albuquerque, and after filling up my gas tank, my next stop was home. But...how about we meet at Quigley Park in about twenty minutes?"

I tiptoe towards my bedroom door and listen. Once safely back on my bed, I say, "See you there."

I throw on a hoodie and grab my house keys in record time.

Fifteen minutes later, I spot Samira's SUV and walk over to meet her. We stroll around the edge of the park, bringing up memories of my grandfather from a couple months ago.

"Is being here too much for you?"

I shake my head. "Nope. We had a nice conversation right here in January."

A toddler runs past us towards the playground, away from his parents sitting on the grass.

It takes Samira a few seconds to respond. "Your grandfather was so grateful to get to know you."

Her kind words hit me right in the heart. Finally.

The dry grass crunches under my feet. "Have people from the mosque been visiting you at home? You're probably not used to being alone..."

"Yes, Muslim sisters from both Albuquerque and Santa Fe have a communal schedule for visits and bringing me dinner." The usual harshness is missing from her voice. "Thank you for asking."

Something really is different. I have no idea where the woman I know is. For an instant, I rethink what I'm about to do. But I push ahead.

"Do you think we could get together and talk about all this legal stuff?"

In my head, I'm counting the ways Samira could shoot my suggestion down, when she says, "That's a good idea.... Would it just be the two of us?"

The little baby hairs on the back of my neck tingle. Lying wouldn't be right. "I haven't asked my mom yet." Pushing away a lingering fear, I ask, "Why? Is that what you want?"

"The three of us really should discuss these things all together, but I'm not excited about a repeat of last time in Mr. Pierce's conference room."

Wow! A step towards normal. I'm crossing my fingers it lasts.

"Do you really want a relationship with us, me AND Mom?"

"Leena, I do. Since the Janaza, when everyone is gone and it's me all by myself in a big house, I've had time to think about you, your mom, and me being the last of the Stewart family. In Islam, you're supposed to treat all people with kindness. I've failed in that. Pain from the past has kept us apart for a long time. Maybe...it's time for my niece and I to fix things."

It sounds good, but I'm not sure. "Really?"

"Yes. So, you and I can get together. Of course, if Asiyah wants to come, then that's fine." Her loud sigh fills my ear.

A huge question keeps nagging at me. "Were you and Tariq really going to marry my mom off to someone when she was sixteen?"

Aunt Samira stops. "We did plan to have a Muslim brother over to meet Asiyah, but your grandfather woke up the next day and canceled it. Neither one of us knew your mom overheard our plans. She ran away before we could explain it to her."

"Maybe it's time you tell her."

Please say yes. Please.

She studies my face. "Maybe you're right."

We're back at the edge of the parking lot. "I should be going. InshaALLAH, I've got an hour drive back to Santa Fe. Leena, thank you for this. You've given me a lot to think about."

Life doesn't suck right now.

Under the setting sun, I step closer and catch her small smile. "Great—I'll talk to my mom about getting together and text you." I tell her. "Thanks for agreeing—I think Tariq would've wanted this."

A sniffle hits my ears. "You understand your grandfather more than you realize. Good night, Leena."

"Bye."

Trying to get my mom to go over to the Stewart house is a hard hill to climb.

With little left to lose, I'm storming ahead.

CHAPTER TWENTY-THREE

March

It's 7 a.m. Saturday—my plan is on.

The dishwasher is empty, and my mom's favorite mug is filled with steaming hot coffee just how she likes it: with three sugars and a splash of creamer. As I pull the last two waffles out of the toaster, the sound of hurried steps turns my head.

"Morning." Her hair is pulled tight into a bun. "This is different." She claims her regular seat. "How long have you been awake?"

Passing her a plate, I say, "Long enough to make us some breakfast and get your daily caffeine habit ready."

"Waffles, tater tots, and a Cutie already peeled—what's the catch?"

Of course she's knows something is up.

After a long sip of room-temperature iced tea, I admit, "I saw Samira last night."

She blows on her coffee but doesn't take a swig. Her hard stare never leaves my face.

When I've bitten my bottom lip twelve times, I say, "Well?"

"You understand my aunt is relentless. She won't stop until you take your shahada. You ready to become a Muslim?"

What if she's right?

Damn, this is harder than I expected.

"Ma, believe it or not, the subject didn't come up." Before she can say something else foul, I continue. "We both agreed to meet and talk about everything in Tariq's will. So... would you consider going with me to your dad's house?"

Instead of an answer, she drums her fingers against the table.

Part of me wants to take it all back.

But my heart refuses to consider the option. "Ma, you won't believe me but Samira wasn't as intense last night—she's trying to change. Nothing like in the lawyer's office."

Mom shakes her head. "Leena, you've known her for a hot minute and are already an expert."

I clear my throat. "Your decisions kept me away from both Tariq and Samira for sixteen years. It's your fault I don't know them better." As soon as the accusation leaves my mouth, I want to disappear like I found Bilbo's precious ring.

Our gazes meet.

The minutes tick away on the digital microwave clock as the silence becomes familiar.

"If I say no, would you still meet with her?" My mom's question is simple but scares the hell out of me.

I scan the empty living room behind her head, looking anywhere but at her.

"Tell me the truth—that's all I've ever asked you to do."

Lifting my gaze slowly, to meet hers, I admit, "I probably would." Searching her face for any sign of anger, I ask, "Is that okay?" Sinking my teeth into my first waffle gives my mouth something to do, but my pulse is still racing.

"One thing I'm not is a hypocrite. Truth between us is how you were raised." She takes a swig of her coffee. "If you insist on doing this, then of course, I'll go with you."

The bright sunshine now streaming into the kitchen gives me hope.

My cheeks hurt but the teeth-baring smile might be permanent. "I'll text Samira and see if she's willing to get together tomorrow."

"Not wasting any time, are you?" She drums her fingertips on the table. "Remember, there's a huge chance this meeting will just continue the chaos between me and Samira—be realistic. My father's sister might have an ulterior motive. Sometimes there are no perfect endings."

"Heard and understood, Ma."

No matter what, it's a chance to get my shrinking family together. One that I have no choice but to take.

Sunday morning, I wake up just after 8 a.m.

After rubbing my eyes, I unlock my phone screen and find Samira's new text. Immediately, I jump out of bed to find my mom. She's opening kitchen cabinets, adding things to a grocery shopping list.

"Ma...Ma, what are you doing this afternoon around four?" I cross the first two fingers of my empty hand.

"Good morning to you too, Leena."

Nobody has time for the smirk on her face. "Mom!"

"Relax. It's too early in the morning for that much energy." After checking the freezer, she says, "If Samira wants to get together, fine. I told you yesterday we'd go together."

Her flat tone isn't even a little positive. But right now, I'll take what I can get.

But when it's time to go, hours later, I'm shocked. Her hair is pulled back into a messy ponytail while her outfit is way too casual.

"Is *that* what you're wearing?"

My mom nods. "If Samira can dress in those floor-length abayas, then she has to accept *my* wardrobe choices. I took a shower and washed my face—what more do you want from me?"

And then we're out the door.

A kaleidoscope of butterflies is bungee jumping in my stomach. My mom turns on the car's heater; in like sixty seconds, sweat dots my forehead. I sneak a look in the passenger-side mirror. My reflection isn't looking good.

An hour later, we pull into the Stewart driveway, right behind the silver Range Rover.

"Let's get this over with." My mom rushes out of the car.

I push out a loud sigh and follow her. Stepping slower than normal, I follow Mom to the front door as my aunt opens it.

"Salaam, Leena, Asiyah. Nice to see both of you." Her smile is surprisingly sweet. "Please come in."

"Hi!" I'm the only who answers her.

Mom pushes her way in. She leaves her sneakers on the shoe rack and looks around the foyer—the hum of the refrigerated air is the only sound anyone can hear.

The living room is exactly the same—there isn't a speck of dust or clutter anywhere. We walk past the leather furniture and into the kitchen. The three of us end up around the island; the cool granite sharpens all five of my senses.

Samira takes out three tall glasses.

"Are you thirsty? We have bottled water, orange juice, or iced tea."

Those are house staples. "I'll have a water. Ma, what about you?"

My mom is silent, her eyes scanning all her surroundings. "Since the iced tea is probably unsweetened, water is fine."

I almost ask how she knows that, but then I get it. "Has it changed a lot since you lived here?"

Samira speaks up. "Since then, the house has been renovated twice. Two years ago, my brother gave me my dream kitchen. I've always loved to cook." She takes chilled waters out of the stainless steel refrigerator's beverage drawer and hands us ours.

"And now, the two of us are part owners of this place. Kind of ironic, isn't it?"

Mom's sharp words don't bring the expected grimace to my aunt's face. Her new calmness is unexpected, close to being unnatural.

After taking a sip of water, my great-aunt says, "Asiyah, your father was always a generous man. Doesn't surprise me at all."

My mom's head turns, her mouth drops open a little as her gaze locks onto Samira.

I'm not the only one surprised.

"Too bad he wasn't as understanding after my mother died." Her hand is squeezing the Fiji bottle so hard, it might explode. "Maybe it wouldn't have been such a toxic environment I had to run away."

"Do you really blame your father for what YOU did?" She points at my mom. "Turning your back on your family, your religion, your entire life, that was all YOU."

Old Samira is back.

Before suffering any more, I bolt out of my bar stool and race into the hallway bathroom. I lean against the back of the locked door, my eyes sliding shut for a second. Muffled voices filter into the space, so I turn on the water. When it's lukewarm, I fill my hands and let the water fall down my face. After shutting off the tap and patting my cheeks dry, I step into the hallway.

Instead of heading back to the kitchen, my feet take me to the doorway of my grandfather's office. I tiptoe into the room, the familiar scent of sandalwood incense greeting me.

"I miss you." The words sound so empty, it's hard to catch my breath. A tiny sliver of my brain thinks I'm extra since we'd only known each other for a short time.

But my heart rules the day.

Walking over to his L-shaped desk brings back the memories when we sat together, me trying to teach him how to use bookmarks. I bite my bottom lip, hoping to stop tears from running down my face.

Not my first failure.

After using the hem of my shirt as a tissue, I see two plain white envelopes on the middle of his desk. One has my name on it, and the other is addressed to my mom.

My hand shakes as I pick up mine.

As I sink into his oversized office chair, my fingers tear open the envelope.

Dearest Leena,
I'm so grateful to have met you. Even though we didn't know each other for many years, you are a Stewart and a wonderful addition to our family. Forgive me for staying away from you and my daughter for all those years.
The past problems are not your fault or because of you. Don't focus on them. You have a bright future ahead of you—I believe

you will find your way and make us all proud. Moving forward, I hope we grow closer and share many memories.
Love, your grandfather.
Tariq

Bringing the single sheet of paper to my chest, I hug his words.

After taking a few minutes to myself, I grab the second envelope and head back to the lion's den, aka the kitchen. Not sure what I'll find there.

"Here." Placing my mom's letter right in front of her brings me a twinge of joy.

"What's this?" She picks up the envelope, studying the handwriting.

After setting down a large platter of green grapes and strawberries, Samira opens a tin of shortbread cookies dusted with powdered sugar. "It's a letter from your father, Asiyah."

Taking advantage of this moment of silence, I help myself to some of the snacks.

"You know about these?" I hold up my letter.

"I do," Samira admits. "Tariq had me look them over after he wrote them a few weeks before he passed."

Mom looks up from the second page of hers; the water pooling in her eyes makes me gasp.

"He let you read this?"

Before my great-aunt could answer, I jump in. "Ma, isn't that a good thing? We are all family here. Family!"

Samira drops a quick "I'll be right back," and she heads down the opposite hallway, towards the bedrooms.

"Are you okay?" Probably a stupid question but I ask anyway.

"I'm not sure." My mom takes a sip of water. "This is a lot right now."

I take a determined first bite of a shortbread cookie—it melts in my mouth. As I go in for bite number two, Samira rejoins us. She hands something to my mom, a book or something.

"Oh my goodness!" She opens the cover. "This is me. Where did you get this photo album?" She shows me the first baby picture of her I've ever seen.

"Is that really Tariq? Where was it taken?" I think it's him, but with darker hair and less laugh lines.

"Yes, it's him, Leena." Samira tells me. Then she points towards the back of the house. "When your mother was a baby, being outside in the fresh air soothed her. A few minutes in the backyard always helped her stop crying."

Checking again, I know it for sure. A much younger version of my grandfather is smiling back at me.

"To answer your question, Asiyah, your father found this about a month before he passed—I thought you might want it."

Math isn't my best subject, but counting has never been one of my struggles.

"That means he wrote our letters AFTER finding your baby pictures." I lean closer to my mom. "Ma, don't you see? Tariq never stopped loving you. Him leaving you something in his will, and now a personal note, proves it."

She leaves her bar stool, then embraces me.

I bury my cheek in her sweatshirt. This moment makes every emotion I've experienced since that first visit to the hospital worth it.

When we finally break apart, my mom says, "Thank you, Samira. You didn't have to give this to me."

"You're welcome, Asiyah."

Seeing the last two members of the Stewart family on friendlier terms, exchanging kind words, is everything. I could get used to this.

CHAPTER
TWENTY-FOUR

July

What the hell was I thinking?

Now that my mom and Samira are getting along, they're coming at me from all sides. With less than a month before my junior year, it makes sense to talk about this now. Doesn't mean I have to like where this conversation is going.

"Just because I have the money to pay for college, doesn't mean it has to be an Ivy League school." Another thought comes to me. "My school has a tutoring service; it's run by seniors."

Neither of them is buying my excuses.

It's way too early in the morning to be double-teamed.

"I think someone who's already finished high school and is a graduate student at UNM is a much better option. Also, having a tutor doesn't mean you can only apply to the top universities—it will help you improve whatever subjects you're struggling with so you're a better candidate to whatever schools you apply to." Samira's explanation is ridiculously obvious.

"I understand the purpose of a tutor but *why* do we have to have one who comes in person?"

Now it's Mom's turn. "You're loaded now. Spending money on top educational practices goes with the territory."

Not knowing if she's serious, I keep my mouth shut.

"Really, Asiyah?" Samira's jaw is hard, then she smiles, her front teeth showing. "Maybe, that's a little bit true."

Now the sides of my mom's mouth are up too. "You're a witness, Leena. She agreed with me."

"What did Rheem say? I know you asked her."

How the hell does she know?

I didn't tell my aunt about how my new friend and I are getting together this week—the topic of college will probably come up.

"Rheem got tutored before, in French. She said it's not a big deal if you choose the right one."

Aunt Samira & Mommy: One
Me: Zero

Watching these two, getting along and *not* engaged in a verbal grudge match, gives me hope for the future. Good thing, because neither of them is budging on the tutoring issue. Once I meet this person Samira found, we'll see if it's a good thing.

My stomach grumbles.

"Let's eat, then we can plan our day." I meet my aunt's eyes. "Are you still okay with spending it with us?"

She nods.

I polish off a whole waffle. Reaching for number two, I notice Samira hasn't touched hers. "Aren't you hungry?"

After taking a sip of her orange juice, she says, "I ate my bacon, but years ago, my brother brought me some Canadian maple syrup back from Quebec—so that's all I've eaten ever since."

"Oh."

Her regular loud voice is closer to a whisper—the memory might be making her sad.

"Don't worry, I got this." My mom heads into the kitchen and returns with take-out sizes of both strawberry jam and honey. "You can use one of these."

I feel my eyes widen as she stares at her options.

"A lot of Muslims use honey, since it's mentioned in the Qur'an, but I don't really like the taste of it," she admits. Samira reaches for the small jar. "I'll try this one. Thank you."

My mom is quick to add, "Be careful, some Muslims might accuse you of heresy."

My aunt smiles, so I do too.

Ten minutes later, her plate is empty.

With three people, cleanup goes faster than normal.

We're all back at the table when my mom says, "Leena, Samira and I talked about this last night when you were out with DeeDee. Would you be okay stopping at the cemetery this morning, to see Tariq's gravestone?"

Her question snatches my regular breath.

Doubts cloud my brain. "Can we bring flowers? Like...is it okay in your faith?" Don't want to mess up things by being disrespectful.

Samira's eyes soften.

"It is more than okay," she says. "It's a very nice gesture."

Mom is more direct. "You're sure about doing this?"

I nod. "Do we have to wear any special clothes or anything?" A headscarf and an abaya is what I'm hinting at but insulting my great-aunt isn't part of the plan.

But she's smiling. "No, I've never heard of a dress code for the cemetery." She points in my direction. "What you're wearing is fine."

The longer I think about it, the less the idea freaks me out. "Since we're all together, we should go."

After stopping at Albertsons for lilies, we head to I25 south. Twenty minutes later, my mom turns in to the cemetery. She switches off the radio.

The happy vibe disappears.

"Turn right and follow the road past the tall piñon pine; that's the Muslim section—park over there." Samira points to a spot up ahead.

We all step out of the car.

I'm stuck in my own thoughts—conversation isn't a possibility for me. My entire body is weighed down; by what, I don't have a clue. My great-aunt leads us to the side of a grave. I don't want to look but do anyway.

Tariq Stewart, Faithful Believer
To ALLAH we belong and to Him we shall return

A steady trickle of water runs down my cheeks. I wipe at it. To my right, Samira has both palms up, reciting something in Arabic. The sound of crunching leaves steals my focus. Glancing around, my mom's now on my left. Her eyes are red, and she's kneeling beside Tariq's gravestone.

"Ma, what are you doing?"

"Just wiping away some dirt."

Such a small thing is too much. I turn away before it breaks me. I race back to the sedan. But I'm not alone for long.

"Leena, are you okay?" Samira lays her hand on my shoulder.

Her eyes are dry, not a tear anywhere on her face.

"Maybe. How many times have you been here?"

She clears her throat. "The first few weeks, I came each Monday and Friday."

My mouth drops open for a second. "Really?"

"I don't have any tears left in my body." She scans the area. "Instead, I make it a point to remember all of my brother's good qualities. He was a great man."

I feel the sides of my mouth turn up. Looking over her shoulder, I notice my mom has my grandfather's letter in her hands. Taking a step in that direction, I swear she's talking to herself.

"Leena, you should stay here. Your mom probably needs some space."

Samira's one hundred percent correct.

My aunt gets back into the back seat while I stand around, leaning against the passenger-side door, feeling the warm sun on my face.

"Leena." My mom's voice forces my eyes open.

"Yes?"

She opens her car door. "Are you ready?"

I nod and get in.

After she's buckled in, Mom asks, "So where are we going?"

I know the perfect place.

"To a bakery. Tariq told me once he loved their ginger cookies, plus they might have the Linzer ones you like, Ma." The twinkle in her eye tells me she agrees.

Samira chimes in from the back seat. "Leena, you want to go there instead of the bookstore?"

As we head to my grandfather's favorite local bakery, I shake my head. "Let's do both."

Combining his fondness for cookies and my obsession with books, it's an appropriate way for us to celebrate the family I always wanted and the one the three of us are building, together.

It's about damn time.

AUTHOR ACKNOWLEDGMENTS:

My Perfect Family was born out of love.

I'm drawn to stories about fraught mother/daughter relationships but wanted to highlight those things in a fractured Black American Muslim family.

My Perfect Family highlights exactly that.

I'm grateful to my kick-ass literary agent, Kristina Perez; my editor, Mora Couch; and everyone at Perez Literary and Holiday House for supporting me and the stories I tell.

To all my writing besties, I appreciate your continuing support and realize how much harder this journey would be without you. Loretta, Alexandra, Laurie, and Jan, merci beaucoup. To my family and close friends, I value all the times you understood the writing took priority.

To the readers, educators, librarians, and those who have positively supported me, I see you and thank you.

Without the Most Generous, the Most Merciful, none of this would've been possible.